'Just let me touch y
murmured

Nora glanced anxiously [...]
ceiling windows.

'No one can see us.' He caressed her all over, lightly, as he kissed her. The sensation was hypnotic, making her feel like a slave to his gradually deepening kisses, his evermore restless touch.

'Trust me.' He took her mouth again, moving in a slow, sinuous rhythm, the rhythm of sex.

Desire thrummed through her. It felt so right, so natural. The temptation to answer his body's sensual dance with her own was nearly too powerful to resist. But resist it she did. 'You said you wouldn't…'

'I'm not going to.'

'This is more than kissing.'

He rolled off her and levered himself up on an elbow. 'So, I gather you've done this before…much as I'd like to believe I'm the first man to ever kiss you…to touch you the way I'm touching you.'

'David, I'm a virgin, not a nun.'

Dear Reader,

Items in newspapers and magazines have inspired several of my books, including this one. I had never heard of 'arm candy' before coming across an article about powerful, well-connected men who attend society functions with stunning young women they have never seen before and will never meet again. These are one-time-only arrangements for the most part, and platonic; at the end of the evening both people go home alone.

Intrigued by the concept, I played the writer's favourite game, 'What If.' What if a brooding sexy Englishman, weary of dating self-serving users, asked a party planner to set him up with 'someone uncomplicated, a model type?' And what if that party planner asked his innocent cousin to go on the date in the guise of a worldly, globe-trotting model, in order to advance his agenda…and hers?

The result is my first Blaze title, *All of Me*, and I hope you have as much fun with it as I did.

Happy reading!

Patricia Ryan

ALL OF ME

by

Patricia Ryan

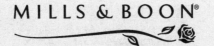

To the inimitable Susan Sheppard,
editor extraordinaire

*MILLS & BOON and MILLS & BOON with the Rose Device
are registered trademarks of the publisher.
Sensual Romance is a registered trademark of
Harlequin Enterprises Limited, used under licence.*

*First published in Great Britain 2000
by Harlequin Mills & Boon Limited,
Eton House, 18-24 Paradise Road, Richmond, Surrey TW9 1SR*

© Patricia Ryan 2000

ISBN 0 263 82406 3

21-1200

*Printed and bound in Spain
by Litografia Rosés S.A., Barcelona*

1

"DO YOU KNOW WHAT arm candy is?" Nora's cousin Harlan asked, juggling her suitcases as he signaled a cab on Seventh Avenue. There'd been a taxi stand right outside Pennsylvania Station, but Harlan had suggested they walk to his place, since it was so close; the heavy luggage had changed his mind.

"Arm candy?" Nora squinted against searing sunshine—a shock to the retinas after the subterranean labyrinth of Penn Station—to take in the pandemonium of midtown Manhattan on this radiant, early September afternoon. "Is that, like, drugs?"

"That's one meaning." He waved a cab over. "What's with the gawking?" The cab swung to a stop in front of them, its trunk popping open when the driver spied the suitcases. Stowing them away, Harlan said, "It's not like you've never been in a big city before."

"Cleveland's minor league compared to this." Nora tossed her army surplus knapsack into the back seat and slid in after it, followed by Harlan, who gave the driver his address in the recently revitalized Manhattan neighborhood of Chelsea. The cab pulled away from the curb into a creeping morass of traffic.

"I get it," Harlan said. "This move to New York is some kind of personal test for you. If you can make it here, you can make it anywhere?"

"Hey, *you* made it here." Nora gave him a playful

punch on the shoulder. Short of stature and graced with a crop of perennially tousled brown hair and an engaging grin, Harlan Armstrong more closely resembled a high school freshman than a successful, self-employed twenty-four-year-old. Seven years ago, when he'd dropped out of high school in their hometown of Keniston, Ohio, population 1,106, and moved to New York, the general opinion was that he would "come to no good." Instead, he'd parlayed his affability and bottomless appetite for la dolce vita into a lucrative career doing something called "events production," which Nora took to be a highfalutin form of party planning.

"So, how's your love life?" she asked, although he was never very forthcoming. "Going steady with anyone?" With his boyish good looks, Harlan had been a girl magnet back at Keniston High, but he'd always balked when it started getting serious.

"'Going steady'? What planet have you been living on?"

The Planet of the Twenty-two-year-old Virgins.

"What about you?" he challenged. "Have you *ever* had a relationship? It can't be—"

Clapping her hands over her ears, Nora sang out, "I can't hear you...nah nah nah nah..."

Harlan pried her hands away. "It can't be for want of opportunity. Men take one look at you, with that blonder-than-blond hair and those legs and that face, not to mention your—" his gaze dropped to her chest "—various other assets, and they get stark raving stupid. Despite this armor of yours," he added, plucking at the jumbo-size sweatshirt she wore over jeans, the shape-concealing uniform she'd adopted when boys had started making more eye contact with her blossoming *assets* than with her.

"That's just it," she said. "Men see the *parts* of me, and they want those parts, but they never want *me*. Not me as a whole person. To them, I'm just a dumb blonde from central casting."

Harlan slapped his forehead. "Don't you get it? It's a vicious circle. Men show some interest in you, and right off the bat, you decide it's not you they want, just your killer bod. The result of which is that you keep them at a distance. Ergo they never get to know the real you, ergo any relationship is nipped in the bud."

"*Ergo?* High school dropouts aren't supposed to salt their conversations with Latin."

"Girls with college degrees in shop aren't supposed to judge other people's—"

"Shop?" Her hard-earned bachelor's degree, which she'd paid for by waiting tables in Cleveland's greasiest rib joint till 2:00 a.m. six nights a week, was in metals, arguably the most challenging crafts major at the Cleveland Institute of Art. "*Shop?*"

"My point," Harlan said with exaggerated patience, "is that someone, somewhere, has got to break that cycle, and given the witlessness of most men when it comes to the finer points of male-female interactions—" he shrugged "—looks like that someone is gonna have to be you, kiddo."

"Advice to the lovelorn from the King of Noncommitment." Yawning, Nora turned and gazed out the window, absorbing the sights and sounds of Manhattan as they scrolled slowly past her field of vision. "So, what's arm candy?"

"Ah. Well. It's, like, a woman who goes out with a man she doesn't know, or doesn't know well, just as sort of...an arrangement. Nothing serious, no romantic involvement whatsoever. Usually some intermediary sets up the date."

"Back home we call them call girls."

"No, no, no," he said quickly. "No sex is involved, and no money is exchanged. The woman is strictly an ornamental date—*ornamental* being the operative word here. These girls, they're the type that really turn heads—professional models, most of them. Tall, gorgeous, with, uh...assets to spare."

"And the men? Older and not quite so ornamental, right?"

"All the men really have in common," Harlan said, "is their position in New York's social food chain, which tends to be right up there with the great white shark. The arm candy is just another status symbol, like their cars or their boats."

"This arm candy deal seems to benefit the sharks a lot more than it does the plankton they're dating," Nora said. "I mean, what do the women get out of it, if there's no money involved?"

"They get to go to A-list events they'd never be invited to otherwise—movie premieres, charity balls, big political receptions. They mingle with big shots they'd ordinarily never get to meet in person."

Nora shrugged. "Seems like a pretty shallow reason for getting all dressed up and pretending to be some stranger's girlfriend. You wouldn't find me going to the trouble."

Harlan addressed her with his most imploring, little-boy look. "Would you go to the trouble as a favor to your cousin who loves you, and is really sorry, but already kind of set it up for you to go to this Red Cross benefit with a really very nice—"

"No."

"Don't say no yet."

"I already said no." A trumpeting of irate car horns made her look out the window to find them ensnared in gridlock. "I mean, honestly, Harlan, can you imagine me all tarted up and hanging on to some guy's arm just to make him look good? *Me*, doing bimbo duty?" She made a face and shuddered.

Harlan contorted himself to pull from the back pocket of his jeans a wad of newspaper, which he smoothed out on his thigh and handed to Nora. "That's him."

Nora peered at a grainy black-and-white image of two men in black tie, both holding champagne flutes. Nora recognized the man on the right as the mayor of New York.

"His name is David Waite," Harlan said, pointing to the man on the left—tall and lean, with black hair and sharply carved features. "Waite with an e. Mid-thirties. He's English—English born, anyway, but I hear he's a confirmed New Yorker now. Studied law at Oxford, and then he kind of dropped off the radar for awhile. Ten-year gap on the résumé."

"Maybe he was in prison. Or a mental hospital."

"Somebody told me he was traveling."

"For ten years?"

Harlan shrugged. "Two years ago, he shows up in New York, rents an office in the Flatiron Building and sets up shop as the Waite Consulting Group, which over-night becomes *the* force to be reckoned with in high-level fund-raising. He represents every big museum, church, health care organization and corporate foundation in New York. What he does is extract donations from the rich and famous in return for a cut of the take. They say he's the best there is."

David Waite's eyes, shadowed by the downward tilt of

his head, were dark and intense. His jaw had a slight thrust to it that, along with the eyes, imparted a hint of ferocity at odds with his debonair attire.

Nora handed the clipping back to her cousin. "No."

"Nora, I need you to do this. It's just for tonight—"

"Tonight?" She wheeled around to face him. *"Tonight?"*

Harlan held his hands up. "I know it's short notice...."

"Do you realize I've spent the last *twelve hours* on a train? It left Cleveland at three-thirty this morning. I've been up for—" she checked her ancient Timex watch "—almost thirty-two hours, and I'm completely burned out. All I can think about is getting to your place and eating something, then crashing."

Mentioning his place reminded Nora that Harlan had offered her the hospitality of his home until she could afford a place of her own. Which, along with the fact that he'd subsidized her nascent jewelry-making venture with an interest-free, pay-it-back-when-you-can loan for supplies—not to mention his unsolicited gifts of cash while she was in college—meant that she owed him. Bigtime. Which he'd be too nice a guy to bring up.

"I'm sorry," Harlan said. "I didn't think about how tired you'd be, just that you'd be in town and could bail me out here."

"Bail you out of what?" she sighed.

Harlan perked up, perceiving, no doubt, that she was teetering atop the slippery slope of capitulation. "This guy, David Waite—I've been wooing his business for a couple of years now. He's the strategic brain behind half the glittery galas and thousand-dollar-a-plate dinners that go on in this town."

"That's a lot of parties," Nora said, catching on.

"He hires event planners, like me, only the people he's

been using..." Harlan shuddered. "Same old hotel ball-rooms, same old food, same old music. I've got ideas out the wazoo, only I'm having a hard time convincing him to take a chance on me, 'cause I'm a little unorthodox. Plus, my experience is mostly with private society af-fairs—weddings, bar mitzvahs. I mean, I do okay, but the really diamond-studded events in this town are the big charity benefits. Anyway, I went to see David at his office this morning, only to find him growling about how he'd canceled his date for the Red Cross benefit—he didn't say why—and that he needed to find some arm candy on a few hours' notice."

Nora glanced at David Waite's handsomely feral vis-age on the clipping in Harlan's hand. "You telling me a guy like that has a hard time finding a date?"

"It's not just a date he wants—it's arm candy. Trust me, David Waite has never wanted for female compan-ionship. The thing is, his taste doesn't generally run to the arm candy type—models, actresses. He tends to go for businesswomen, professional women, that sort. But tonight, for whatever reason, he wants to walk in with Barbarella on his arm."

"Is that why he canceled his date for tonight? Because she wasn't Barbarella? That's pretty obnoxious."

"I have no idea why he canceled it. It's tacky to inter-rogate someone you're toadying up to. All I know is, he asked me if I could find him someone presentable but un-complicated—'a model type' is how he put it—and being the opportunistic pilot fish that I am, I told him no prob-lemo."

"Why you?"

"Event producers sooner or later meet just about ev-erybody there is to meet, and we never lose a phone number. Need a sword swallower? A graffiti artist? A company of ballerinas? A crew of waiters willing to dress up in bunny costumes? A little arm candy? All I've got to do is make a phone call."

"So you volunteered me for the job?"

"Actually, the person I had in mind was this really hot runway model, but it turns out she's been in rehab for the past month. I didn't panic, 'cause I knew a few other models, but they all had plans for the evening or were out of town on bookings. Which leaves you."

"I'm not a model."

"You could pass. I *need* you, Nora. I've already promised Waite I'd find him a date. If I come up empty, he'll think I'm all talk and will never hire me, and my career will stall out right where it is until the end of time."

She knew she should help him. She wanted to help him. But... "Isn't there *anybody* else who could do this?"

"I can't set this guy up with just anybody. It's gotta be someone absolutely jaw-dropping. You clean up pretty good, as I recall. I don't suppose you brought any evening gowns with you."

"Sure, they're right in here—" Nora patted her knapsack "—along with my rhinestone tiaras and long silk gloves."

"Not to worry. I know how we can get you fixed up."

"How reassuring." She slumped down in the seat. "Oh, God, Harlan, I don't know if I can do this."

"Sure you can." Harlan stuffed the clipping back into his pocket. "Hey, you'll be partying down with the cream of New York society your first night in town." He tapped on the cab's plexiglass partition. "Right here is fine."

"Here?" Nora looked around in dismay as she unfolded herself from the cab. They'd pulled up in front of what appeared to be some sort of grim old factory or warehouse in a tumbledown industrial neighborhood. "I thought you had money."

"I do. That's how I could afford to buy the whole top floor of this building. Keep the change," he said, handing some bills to the driver and retrieving her suitcases from the trunk. The cab drove away, street litter swirling in its wake. Harlan carried her bags to the front door and opened it with a key.

She slung her knapsack over one shoulder and followed him down a narrow hallway and into an enormous old freight elevator with a rusty metal sliding door and an expandable iron gate, both of which had to be pulled shut by hand. Harlan punched a button and the antiquated conveyance groaned and clattered up to the sixth floor, opening onto a dreary little vestibule featuring a brown-painted steel door with a peephole, an incinerator shaft and a single exposed lightbulb dangling overhead.

I've made a terrible mistake, coming to New York, Nora thought. *A terrible, terrible, terrible mistake.*

"Don't judge the place till you've seen the inside." Harlan twisted a key in the first of many formidable-looking locks encrusting the brown door. He could always read her mind.

"Harlan?" called a man's voice from within the apartment.

Locks chunked in rapid succession, and then the door swung open, courtesy of a thirtyish, fair-haired man clad in black jeans and a black T-shirt. "If it isn't Nora of Sunnybrook Farm!" Throwing his arms around her, he kissed her on both cheeks. "Come in, come in, come in!" He led her by the hand into a sprawling living room where antiques and Oriental rugs were nearly lost amid a riotous jungle of exotic plants. A jazz piano piece wafted softly from invisible speakers; massive pillar candles scented the air with whispers of vanilla and honeysuckle. Nora felt like Dorothy encountering a kaleidoscopic Munchkinland after bleak old monochromatic Kansas.

Closing the door with a kick as he hauled the suitcases into the apartment, Harlan said, "Nora, this is Kevin Mills. Kevin, what are you doing here? I thought rehearsal went until five."

"I cut out early so I could be here to meet and greet." Kevin plucked at Nora's knapsack. "No offense, but you carry this in public? Honey, this is for keeping your gear dry when you're on a forced march through forty miles of rice paddies. Harlan, where are we putting her? We never decided."

We? "Oh," Nora said. "Harlan, I didn't realize you had a roommate. Kevin, are you sure it's all right for me to stay here? I don't want to impose."

"Sweetie, of course you're not imposing." Kevin patted her cheek with a hand that felt just a tad too soft to be a man's. His blond hair, she noted, was styled to look fetchingly mussed, and had dark roots that she took to be a fashion statement.

Could Kevin be gay? she wondered, and instantly concluded that he could and he was. Did Harlan know?

"So, where are we going to put her?" Kevin asked Harlan. "I mean, there's just the one bed, and even though it's king-size, I'd say three would be a bit of a crowd in there, wouldn't you?"

It would appear, Nora realized with a dull shock, that Harlan knew. She stared incredulously at her cousin as his face bloomed with color.

"Oops," Kevin said.

"Uh, Kevin," Harlan said, "you think you could

maybe scrounge up something for Nora to eat? Nora, come with me."

Nora followed numbly as Harlan, still carrying her bags, guided her through the warmly decorated apartment. Holding aside a lush curtain of vines cascading from hanging pots, he gestured her into a cavernous, high-ceilinged room flooded with sunshine from countless skylights and punctuated by columns. The vast space was further partitioned by industrial shelving bearing what she took to be Harlan's professional accoutrements: rows of vases, urns, buckets, tubs and troughs for holding flowers; stacks of table linens in a rainbow of hues; hundreds of candelabras in every size and shape imaginable; garlands of silk orange blossoms; African drums; feathered headdresses; glittery disco balls; strings of fairy lights; Mardi Gras masks, Kabuki masks, monster masks....

"Holy cow," Nora murmured.

"My parties involve more props than most Broadway shows."

He led her through a sun-washed copse of faux marble columns and latticework trellises; ersatz Greek statuary, mostly of half-naked gods and goddesses; rolls of satin bunting; suits of armor; papier-mâché farm animals; backdrops painted like formal gardens, snow-capped mountains, Paris at night; tents, tepees, pyramids, gazebos, pagodas...even a flying saucer with eerily realistic aliens peering out through the windows.

At the rear of the huge space, she discovered a wall of windows fitted with yellowish rice-paper shades, rolled to reveal a postcard-perfect, late-afternoon view of the Manhattan skyline. A little observation area had been set up on a big braided rug: a cast-iron daybed pressed into service as a couch via heaps of pillows, a pair of brass floor lamps flanking it and, in lieu of a coffee table, an ancient cedar chest on which sat a battered old milk bucket filled with dried wheat, which ambushed Nora with an unexpected surge of homesickness for rural Ohio.

To one side of this makeshift sitting area stood rows of portable clothes racks hung with what looked liked dresses.

"Those are Kevin's costumes." Harlan set her suitcases next to the daybed and rolled his shoulders. "He handles wardrobe and makeup for an off-Broadway play down the street—*Two Little Exes*. It's got an all-male cast, but they portray female archetypes—everyone from Lizzie Borden to Snow White to Courtney Love."

"It's a drag show."

"It's a rock musical, and it happens to have gotten rave reviews from none other than the *New York Times*."

"Hunh." *We're definitely not in Kansas anymore, Toto.*

"I thought you could bunk back here," Harlan said.

"Uh…" She was supposed to sleep here, in this Museum of Oddities and Curiosities, tripping over aliens and medieval knights and Greek gods on the way to the bathroom in the middle of the night? "Okay. Fine. Great. Can't beat the view."

"Hey, and starting next Saturday, you'll have the entire place to yourself for two weeks. Kev and I are going to the Caribbean."

"Really?" Nora said in a small voice. She'd be living here in this surrealistic apartment in the middle of this immense, terrifying city *all alone?*

"Oh—I was thinking we could clear out an area back here near the windows for you to make your jewelry. I arranged to get you a worktable with a vise and an acetylene torch and that other stuff you asked for. It's coming tomorrow."

"That's sweet of you. I really appreciate it."

"Anything for my favorite cousin."

She dumped her knapsack on the daybed. "So, how long have you known you were gay, and did it just kind of slip your mind that you never bothered to mention it to me?"

He closed his eyes briefly. "I can't remember a time when I didn't at least suspect. But I was afraid that if I told anybody in Ohio, even you, sooner or later it'd end up on the front page of the *Keniston Post-Register*—Local Boy Doomed to Hell—and I'd never be able to show my face at home again."

"You had to know I'd figure it out the second I got here."

"Sure, but I also knew you'd be *here*, in New York, on my home turf, not back in Ohio, where you might inadvertently let something slip to the wrong person. I'm sorry, Nora. I should have told you a long time ago. Are we still pals?"

She smiled crookedly. "How could we ever not be pals?"

He gathered her into a hug. "You had me worried there."

A trilling sound arose from somewhere between them.

Harlan said, "Either we're making beautiful music together, or that's my cell phone."

"My money's on the cell phone."

He withdrew the phone from inside his jacket and flipped it open. "Harlan Armstrong." His eyes widened fractionally; he glanced at Nora. "David! Good to hear from you."

David Waite? Nora groaned.

"Here you are!" Kevin emerged from the forest of ar-

cane party props bearing a tray of sandwiches and bot-
tled water.

"I'm lookin' at her right now," Harlan said into the
phone, his tone hearty and reassuring. "All systems are
go."

"*What?*" Nora exclaimed in a stage whisper, suddenly
terrified at the prospect of playing arm candy to David
Waite. "*No!*"

Harlan turned his back to her. "Oh, yeah, she's into it.
Did I, uh...did I happen to mention that she's my
cousin?"

Nora circled Harlan and seized the sheepskin collar of
his jacket, furiously shaking her head.

Harlan gave her an imploring look and mouthed
Please. "Mislead you?" he said. "No, David, no—of
course I didn't mislead you. She *is* a model—Nora Armstrong's her name. She's, uh, she's staying with me,
'cause she just got back into town from..." Harlan
wagged a hand and looked around helplessly.

"Tahiti." Kevin set the tray of sandwiches on the chest.

"Tahiti." Harlan rubbed his forehead. "Uh, some sort
of...swimsuit layout, I think. One of those calendars,
maybe."

"Harlan..." Nora began.

Harlan slapped a hand over her mouth. "Hmm? No,
she, uh, doesn't actually have a place of her own. Not
anymore. 'Cause, uh...she was out of town for awhile.
She's been working in..." He looked toward Kevin ex-
pectantly.

"Milan."

"Milan."

Nora yanked his hand away. "Milan? Tahiti? Harlan..."

"Why don't you tell her yourself?" Handing the phone

to Nora, Harlan dropped to his knees, clasped his hands in prayerful supplication and mouthed, *Please please please please please.*

"Miss Armstrong?" The voice on the other end of the line was deep and softly rough, like Shetland wool.

"Uh...y-yes?"

"I wanted to tell you how much I appreciate your doing this, especially on such short notice." Waite had one of those well-bred *Masterpiece Theatre* accents that, along with that gently rumbling voice, made him sound like God.

Or at least like Jeremy Irons.

Nora swallowed. "Thank you. I mean, you're welcome."

"And, of course, I'm grateful to your cousin for having set this up," Waite continued, the remote politeness of his tone a chilly contrast to that swoon-inducing voice.

That's the whole idea, Sherlock. You're supposed to be grateful. "Yeah, he's a real helpful guy," Nora muttered, pondering the ways in which she herself was indebted to Harlan, and the fact that he'd never asked for anything in return for all this bounty. Nothing. Until now.

"Shall I come round for you at half past eight, then?"

Harlan clutched at her legs and gave her the ol' puppy-dog eye. "Half past eight would be fine," she said woodenly.

Her cousin slumped against her, closed his eyes and breathed, "Thank you, thank you, thank you."

"I'll see you then," Waite said.

The phone clicked as Nora was saying, "Goodbye."

"Nora, thank you!" Shooting to his feet, Harlan wrapped her in his arms and kissed her soundly on the cheek. "I love you!"

"Really? 'Cause I'm growing to hate you." She collapsed on the daybed and took a sandwich. Roast beef, way too rare. She'd heard New Yorkers ate their meat raw. It went back on the tray.

"She's sleeping here?" Kevin asked. "I didn't think she'd like it here, surrounded by all your Felliniesque effluvia."

"She doesn't." Harlan grabbed a sandwich as he plopped down next to her. "She feels vulnerable and exposed without four tidy little walls around her, but she's too polite to say anything."

"*Will* you stop reading my mind?" Nora snapped.

"Four walls, huh?" Crossing to the nearest dress rack, Kevin pulled it across the floor until it was positioned at the edge of the braided rug. He did the same with the rest of the racks, setting them up in a squared-off border around three sides of the little sitting area, the fourth being the wall of windows, with a narrow gap in one corner to serve as a sort of doorway. "Voilà! Four walls."

Harlan looked toward Nora for her reaction as he chewed.

"Cool," she said with a smile, and meant it. "Thanks, Kevin." By moving aside the dress racks, he'd exposed wire storage units filled with wigs and shoes, as well as a sewing machine on a table near the windows. "Did you make all these costumes?" she asked him.

"Some." He cracked open a bottle of water. "The rest I bought, but they usually have to be altered to fit a guy."

"Speaking of which," Harlan said around a mouthful of sandwich, "Nora's going to be needing an evening gown for tonight, something sexy but elegant. Plus shoes, hair, makeup, the works. I was hoping you could wield that magic wand of yours and do a Cinderella transformation on our country cousin here."

"A little Fairy Godmother action, huh?" Kevin spread

his arms wide. "A role I was born to play! You're what, about five feet ten, right?" he asked Nora. "What's your dress size?"

"Uh..." The wardrobe manager for a cross-dressing rock musical was going to give her a makeover? Visions of beehive hairdos and purple eyeshadow danced in her head.

"Wait, let me guess." Standing up, he pulled Nora to her feet and scrutinized her, head to toe. "This bag lady getup doesn't help, but I'd say...a ten on top and eight on the bottom." With the air of a man who'd made an executive decision, he plucked a gown off a rack and held it up for her inspection.

"That?" Nora said. It was a floor-length slip of bias-cut silk the color of copper, suspended from its padded satin hanger by means of threadlike spaghetti straps. Kevin spun the hanger around to show off the garment's drastically scooping back.

"There's nothing to it," she protested, unnerved at the prospect of trading in her plus-size comfort clothes for a little whisper of silk so insubstantial it could be crushed in one hand.

"There will be once you've got it on." Kevin smiled. "It's perfect."

Perfect, Nora mused, for displaying charms she'd made a career out of camouflaging. Perfect for a role she'd long ago decided she wanted no part of. What was wrong with this picture?

"Try it on." Harlan rose and unfurled the rice-paper shades over the windows, casting the space into a buttery soft twilight.

Kevin's gaze zeroed in on her chest. "You're what, about a thirty-six C? I've got a nice backless, strapless, long-line push-up bra that'll give you even more to love, and it comes with a matching thong."

"Thong!" Nora squirmed just thinking about it.

"Panty lines are the kiss of death with a dress like this. I've got some fabulous zirconium jewelry that looks just like the real thing. And if you wear a size nine shoe, and I'll bet my eyelash curler you do, I've got some gold stilettos to die for."

"If I can walk in them, I'll take them," Nora said, "but I'll pass on the jewelry. I only wear my own."

Unbuckling her knapsack, she withdrew her most spectacular necklace—a loop of gold made to look like a wreath of branches, from which dangled two dozen smoothly polished chunks of amber, onyx and garnet. In the center, lower than the rest, she'd hung the "eagle's egg"—a large, ovoid nugget of amber encasing the body of a prehistoric winged insect so perfectly preserved that it could have passed for one of her father's fishing flies.

The necklace rattled softly as Kevin took it from her and held it in front of the window. "This," he pronounced earnestly as he peered through the myriad translucent stones, "is the ugliest thing I've ever seen."

Harlan draped a brotherly arm over Nora's shoulders. "Don't mind him, kiddo. He's got an embarrassing penchant for flash and glitter. It's his only major flaw."

"That," Kevin said, "and a weakness for men who apologize for me when they should be trying to talk their beloved cousins out of accessorizing silk evening gowns with rocks and bugs. Here." Holding the necklace with two fingers, he handed it back. "Try the dress on so I can mark it. Then you can take a nice, relaxing whirlpool bath while I alter it, and afterward I can do your hair and makeup." Her alarm must have shown on her face, because he added, "I promise not to turn you into Ru Paul."

Nora ordered the men to wait outside the dress-rack perimeter while she changed, over Kevin's protests that they were quite immune to her charms. She unzipped her sweatshirt while Harlan launched into a lecture on arm candy protocol.

"The thing to remember about tonight," he said, "is that you're there strictly for David Waite's benefit. You're an adornment. Stick close to him, smile a lot, laugh at his jokes. Be charming, agree with everything he says, but don't talk too much, and don't do too much socializing on your own."

"You're turning me into a geisha." She tossed aside the sweatshirt and started tugging off her T-shirt.

"No, I told you—there's no sex involved."

"Geishas aren't prostitutes," Kevin said, "not really."

"That's right." She sat on the daybed to untie her Keds. "Their job is to look good and pamper men, that's all. They, like, serve tea and sing and stuff."

"Oh, and don't let on to anyone that you just met him," Harlan said, "'cause then they'll know you're arm candy. The idea is for people to think you've got something going with him."

"Why doesn't he just take one of those blow-up party dolls," Nora asked, "and be done with it?"

"Nora..."

"You do realize I'm majorly exhausted tonight." She shimmied out of her jeans and kicked them aside. "You know how bitchy I get when I haven't gotten enough sleep."

"You?" Kevin exclaimed. "Bitchy?"

"Yeah, she's got a real short fuse when she's tired," Harlan said. "Nora, honey, just promise me you'll think before you speak tonight. Please. Oh, and don't let him know you make jewelry. He thinks you're a model. If anyone asks what agency you're with, say 'Boss.' Boss Models Worldwide, I think it's called. If they ask how much you're getting paid, say—"

"Nobody would be that rude." Nora settled the necklace over her shoulders and reached beneath her braid to fasten it. As always, she reveled in the weight of the warm, heavy stones against her chest.

"This is New York," Harlan said. "They're that rude. Tell them you make five thousand dollars a day."

"A *day?*"

She slid the gown on, shivering as it glided cool and sleek, over her skin. "I don't think I can say that with a straight face." Nora raised one of the window shades to inspect her reflection in the glass. It was a stunning dress, but her bra straps and disheveled hair made her look like a seven-year-old who'd gotten into her mother's closet. No matter how skillfully Kevin made her over, she'd still be a Midwestern farm girl playing dress-up. An impostor. "This evening is shaping up to be an ulcer in the making."

"Oh, sweetie, you'll do fine," Kevin interjected. "Don't listen to Harlan. Just relax and have a good time."

"No!" Harlan said. "Don't relax! Stay on your toes. Too much is at stake here. Oh, uh...I don't want to insult you or anything, but you know which fork to use, and all that, right?"

"The pitchfork is for hay, the tuning fork is for pianos."

Harlan sighed. "Nora, remember—you just got back from a photo shoot in Tahiti, and before that, you were living in Milan. Can you remember all that? Five thousand a day, Tahiti—"

"What if I can't? Will your life be ruined?"

"Just my career," he said with a drawn-out sigh.

Nora scowled at her image in the window, superimposed over a golden, late-afternoon panorama of the city she'd dreamed about moving to for years, and now almost wished she'd never set foot in. "I *have* mentioned that I hate you, right?"

THE DOWNSTAIRS DOORBELL chimed as Kevin was putting the finishing touches on Nora's makeup at the big antique, gold-framed mirror over the bathroom sink. He tossed the eyebrow brush back in his toolbox full of cosmetics and checked his watch. "He's punctual. How unexpectedly banal."

Nora's stomach clutched. *What am I doing? This is nuts.*

The bathroom door whipped open; Harlan popped his head through. "He's here! I just buzzed him in. Are you ready?"

"Just about," Kevin said.

"What about my hair?" Nora asked.

"Give me five minutes." Kevin produced a curling wand from his box of tricks and plugged it in.

"You remember everything I told you, right?" Harlan asked her. "Stick close to David, don't talk too much—"

"Harlan, do you hover and panic this much when you're planning one of your parties?" she asked through a yawn.

"Yes. That's why everything always goes off without a hitch." He scowled at her mouth. "Kev? You really think that's the right shade of lipstick? Wouldn't something darker—"

"Stop micromanaging," Kevin said as he rubbed a dab of hair gel into her eyebrows, "and get out there. He's going to be at the door—" three sharp raps sounded at the apartment door "—right about now."

"Show time." Harlan walked away, leaving the door

ajar. In a moment, there came the *chunk-chunk-chunk* of locks disengaging, followed by the soft *screek* of the front door opening. Nora eavesdropped unashamedly while Kevin brushed a light dusting of iridescent powder over the crests of her cheekbones.

"David!" Harlan's voice was muffled but clearly audible. "Nice to see you again."

"Harlan."

Hearing David Waite's *Brideshead Revisited* voice so near filled Nora with a cold, thrumming panic.

"Can I take your coat?" Harlan offered.

"I'll keep it, thanks. She's ready, I hope. I did say half past eight."

"Oh, she's ready," Harlan assured him, adding too loudly, for her benefit, "She'll be right out."

Nora gazed heavenward. *I should have my head examined.*

"Relax." Kevin dabbed oil from a tiny glass bottle labeled Lavender onto the bristles of a boar's-hair brush. "You look like you're getting psyched up for a lethal injection."

"He intimidates me."

"Nora, look at yourself." Kevin raised her chin, forcing her to confront her reflection in the mirror.

Nora had, indeed, cleaned up pretty good tonight. Her makeup, which Kevin had applied with a surprisingly deft and subtle hand, enhanced her features in a way she'd never quite been able to pull off herself. He'd taken the dress in just a stitch here and there, until it floated at a distance of exactly one micron from her body, making her look as if she'd been dipped in melted pennies. The bra he'd given her to wear snugged her breasts up just enough to produce a luxuriant cleavage, in which the eagle's egg nestled cozily.

Provocative but polished, every detail impeccable. The very essence of a geisha. Nora smiled and the illusion was complete.

"If anyone will be intimidated tonight," Kevin announced as he brushed out her hair, "it'll be David Waite."

In the living room, Harlan was inviting David to have a seat and offering him a drink.

"Scotch, if you've got it," Waite said, defrosting somewhat.

"Neat?"

"Rocks. Mind if I smoke?"

"Not at all, not at all. I, uh...I'm sure I have something around here you can use as an ashtray."

Kevin smirked into the mirror. "Harlan's normally the first one to tell them to take it outside. Makes me cringe to see him grovel this way."

He gathered Nora's hair into a gleaming sheaf and twisted it into a coil, which he secured at her nape by piercing it with two jeweled and feathered picks from her own collection of handmade hair ornaments. Some wayward tendrils sprang loose around her face and neck, and these he touched up with the curling wand. The result was both sophisticated and ingenuous.

He turned her around and gave her a critical once-over, his gaze lingering on the necklace. "It's growing on me. Doesn't look half as gruesome as it did this afternoon."

"You scare me when you say things like that, Kevin. I came to New York to establish a *business* making jewelry like this. I've got to cultivate patrons, build a clientele of people who *like* this kind of thing." Although how she would actually do that, considering the one-of-a-kind nature of her work and its costliness, remained to be seen.

"Oh, don't let me get to you, sweetie. Like Harlan said, I'm a slave to flash and glitter. Speaking of which—" he lifted her unmanicured hands and eyed them critically "—there's still time for press-ons. I'm quick."

Nora shuddered. "I've got to draw the line somewhere."

Kevin held the door open. "You're on. I'll go get your bag and jacket."

Willing herself not to nibble her painstakingly lipsticked lips—mochaccino pink layered with a sheen of copperglaze frost—Nora squared her shoulders and walked past the bedroom and kitchen, listening intently. Harlan and David Waite were sharing observations on the New York social scene, their conversation relaxed and amiable. Waite even chuckled once or twice, which she found gratifying. Maybe he really was a nice guy, as Harlan seemed to think, and not the stone cold piece of work he'd come off as during their phone conversation.

At the edge of the living room, she paused behind some potted ficus trees to peer through their leaves. Harlan and Waite, seated on matching brown velvet chairs, faced each other across a massive marble-topped coffee table. Waite had his back to her; all she could see of him was a head of black hair and a wisp of smoke curling toward the ceiling.

"Where are you holding this benefit tonight?" Harlan asked.

"The Waldorf." Ice cubes clinked softly as Waite sipped from his drink.

"Empire Room?"

"Grand Ballroom."

Harlan's eyebrows rose. "I'm impressed."

Waite tapped his cigarette into the cut glass candy dish

that was substituting for an ashtray. "We needed a room that size. It seats fifteen hundred for banquets."

"It's a spectacular room," Harlan said. "Perfect for when you want an aura of old-world heaviosity. But have you ever thought about—now, keep an open mind—a parking ramp?"

An incredulous little huff of laughter escaped from Waite. "You mean a public garage?" he asked, pronouncing it *gar*age.

"No, no, no, it wouldn't *look* like a garage," Harlan quickly added. "Not inside. I'd do it up like the interior of a medieval castle, or maybe an Egyptian tomb filled with treasure and secret passageways, or—"

"I'll take it under advisement." Waite set his glass on the table and checked his watch. "Are you sure she's ready?"

"Or we could use an airplane hanger, or a warehouse," Harlan persisted. "You could even bus people out of town, to a winery, or maybe a casino. I'm talking a different kind of event here, one that would appeal to people my age, Generation X types."

"The children of the old guard? They tend to be self-centered, and therefore cheap—long pockets and short arms."

"Forget the trust fund kids. There are entrepreneurs in fields like computing and telecommunications, fresh-faced kids with bulging pockets who'd jump at the chance to empty them for a good cause—if only they were approached the right way. Black-tie charity balls don't do it for them. Oh—the Bronx Zoo. How about that? Or a theme park, or a racetrack, or—"

Now. Nora stepped out from behind the thicket of ficus, silencing Harlan in mid sales pitch.

"Nora." Harlan leapt to his feet, his gaze sweeping

over her with obvious approval. "Let me introduce David."

Leaning forward, David Waite stubbed his cigarette out in the candy dish, stood and turned to face her.

Her first thought was that he was bizarrely tall—a giant in black tie beneath an open black-velvet-collared topcoat draped with a white silk scarf—but then, Harlan made most men look tall by comparison. Nevertheless, David still topped Nora in her five-inch heels, which put him at several inches over six feet.

Her second thought was that he was almost absurdly handsome, his dark blue eyes deep set and piercing, his face sculpted in keen-edged planes. His inky hair was just slightly untidy, as if he'd run a restless hand through it after taking the trouble to comb it out neatly.

All in all, the very image of an evening-wear model for *GQ:* urbane, civilized, but still very much the stone hunk.

There seemed to be the briefest, most ephemeral kindling of something in his gaze—an interest more primeval than civilized—as he took her in. It was gone in a blink, replaced by an impenetrable civility, leaving her to wonder if she'd just imagined it. Had it merely been wishful thinking?

Right. Interest of that sort from David Waite was the last thing she should wish for. This was a cold-blooded business arrangement tonight, a one-shot favor to Harlan—nothing more. That was just how she wanted it, of course; she hated it when men lusted after the package she came in without ever bothering to look inside. If she'd been subconsciously wishing for some sort of reaction from Waite, it was because of all the trouble she and Kevin had gone to, fashioning this silk purse out of the proverbial sow's ear.

"Nora," Harlan said, "this is David. David, Nora."

Waite stepped forward and extended his hand. "Miss Armstrong."

Ah, so he was opting for brisk formality. Good.

"Mr. Waite." She smiled politely as she shook his hand.

"You kids have a good time tonight." Kevin strode in bearing a gold brocade evening jacket and mesh purse. "Honey, did you give them the car keys?" he asked Harlan.

With a look of forbearance, Harlan introduced Waite to Kevin, who took a set of house keys from his pocket, dropped them into the purse and handed it to Nora.

As she was opening up the jacket to put it on, Waite stepped forward and held a hand out. "Allow me."

Unused to such courtly gestures, Nora hesitated slightly before handing over the jacket. Standing behind her, Waite held it open so she could slide her arms into the satin-lined sleeves. He drew the jacket up, the backs of his fingers raising a path of shivery goose bumps as they grazed the bare flesh of her arms.

As she shrugged into the jacket, its beaded lapels turned partially inward. Coming around to face her, Waite adjusted them so that they lay flat. Nora breathed in a hint of something warmly aromatic—aftershave, probably—mingled with a whisper of tobacco. Unsure where to look, she stared at his hands. Devoid of rings, the nails bluntly cut, they might have been the hands of a laborer—although it seemed to her that there was something vaguely aristocratic about the unusual length of his fingers.

Aristocratic and sensual. *David Waite has never wanted for female companionship*, Harlan had said.

She looked up and met his dark, unwavering gaze.

It's true, she thought helplessly. *I made a terrible, terrible mistake, coming to New York.*

2

"YOU'RE YAWNING AGAIN." David set his empty coffee cup on the saucer next to his untouched napoleon. Not only was she yawning, but her eyes had grown increasingly heavy-lidded as the evening progressed, lending them a seductively slumberous quality that was all too hard to look away from.

Nora winced slightly. "I thought I was hiding those yawns pretty well." She had a bedroom voice, throaty and a little kittenish, as if she'd just awoken to her lover's touch.

"You have been." But he'd been watching her, and more attentively than she probably realized. How could he not? Of the hundreds of women at this affair tonight, Nora Armstrong was by far the most beautiful. In truth, she was astoundingly, almost unnervingly beautiful, a statuesque silver-blonde with a face to rival any of her competitors in the world of modeling—extravagant cheekbones, a heart-stopping smile and wide hazel eyes that looked right at him, direct and knowing.

That was the unnerving part, the forthright gaze. It was a rarity in the higher echelons of New York society, where one's dinner companion often spent the meal scanning the room for more prestigious company whilst perfunctorily holding up her end of the conversation.

Nora's attire—a lustrous sheath of coppery silk embellished with a primitive but spectacularly beautiful necklace—conspired to enhance her natural beauty with a dash of the untamed. The necklace kept drawing his attention, not only because it was really quite striking—like something unearthed from a hidden tomb—but because it rested on one of the lushest, most creamy-skinned bosoms he'd ever seen. There seemed to be something imbedded in the large chunk of amber that served as the necklace's centerpiece—an insect, perhaps? Cursing the prematurely declining vision that had him in reading glasses at the tender age of thirty-four, David resisted the urge to squint in the direction of her breasts like some spotty schoolboy.

She reminded him of those Balinese twin sisters who'd danced the *legong* for him that long-ago night by the light of palm-oil lamps, hypnotizing him with their smoky eyes and sinuous, ritualized movements. The illusion of Nora Armstrong as pagan enchantress was intriguingly at odds with her current surroundings—the upper tier of the Waldorf-Astoria's opulent, four-story Grand Ballroom.

Tonight's benefit having drawn, to his gratification, as many people as the ballroom could seat for dinner, both the upper tier and the main floor it overlooked were a sea of pink-linened tables with lavish floral centerpieces. A hundred fifty tables in all, each seating five elegantly garbed couples who'd contributed generously to the American Red Cross for the privilege of being here. Some were philanthropic by nature. Others had to be bullied into giving, or did it to advance themselves socially. Then there were those who gave simply because that was their entrée to the most prestigious social events in New York.

This particular do had been a rousing success, but it was coming up to midnight, and the festivities were in the process of winding down. The speech making was long since over, and now, on the ballroom's velvet-curtained stage, a gawky adolescent musical prodigy played Beethoven sonatas at a gleaming grand piano. Fifteen hundred excellent meals had been eaten and cleared away by an army of well-trained servers, who continued to circulate with coffee and champagne, although people were already starting to leave. In fact, David and Nora were the only ones left at their table.

Nora hid yet another yawn behind her hand, the nails of which were short and unvarnished; must be a new fashion trend.

"Are you that bored?" he asked her. When they'd first arrived at the Waldorf she'd seemed just the opposite, taking in everything—the sumptuous surroundings, the glittery crowd, the pomp and circumstance—with unblinking interest. She'd kept to his side, appropriately quiet and unassuming, as he'd roamed among the guests, touching base with his clients and networking with the most influential patrons. During the speeches, she'd listened attentively, and when dinner was served, she'd tucked into it with gusto. The healthy appetite had surprised him, given her membership in a notoriously food-phobic profession. But then, she was a good deal more generously proportioned than most of her painfully thin colleagues, who tended to look more like adolescent boys than grown women.

"I'm not bored," she said, poking the brittle, cream-filled layers of her napoleon with a fork, as if pondering how to consume it without making it shatter into a gooey mess. "Just tired, is all. I was up all night."

"Ah." No doubt club-hopping till dawn. Models tended to be world-class party animals, and it would appear that the lovely Miss Armstrong was no exception. "This obviously isn't your sort of crowd."

"My sort of crowd?" Substituting her fingers for the fork, she pried off the napoleon's entire top stratum, a sheet of puff pastry coated on one side with powdered sugar and on the other with custard. "What's my sort of crowd?"

David summoned a waiter weaving between the tables with a tray of full champagne flutes. "Rock stars and those with pretensions thereof, eurotrash with titles no one cares about anymore, models who fancy themselves aspiring actors, perhaps the occasional vacuous young socialite or peddler of the newest designer drug, and various hangers-on of the aforementioned. In short, anyone whose idea of an evening well spent is laying waste to a hotel room. Am I close?"

She held the sheet of pastry to her mouth and took a tentative lick, the tip of her tongue scooping up the tiniest dollop of custard, which she tasted with half-closed eyes. Meeting his gaze, she smiled. "You're not even warm."

Any warmer and he'd spontaneously combust. David took two glasses from the waiter's tray and handed one to Nora. "Cheers."

Nora took a sip of her own and smiled. "I shouldn't drink this, 'cause it'll only make me sleepier, but I just love the way the bubbles tickle my nose."

She seemed more relaxed now that they were alone than she had during dinner, when she'd been obliged, along with him, to make small talk with their tablemates. They'd been a congenial group, mostly acquaintances of David's, and decent conversationalists, but Nora had spoken only when directly addressed, and then she'd seemed strangely guarded. Perhaps she simply didn't know how to converse with people twice her age whose interests weren't limited to the latest hot new band or whether navy would be the new black next season.

"Perhaps I missed the mark when it comes to your sort of crowd," he conceded, "perhaps not. But you certainly seemed to find our dinner companions tiresome."

"Actually, I kind of liked those people." She nibbled one corner off the confection she was devouring with such lingering relish, washing it down with a generous swallow of champagne.

"Really? You seemed decidedly ill at ease to me. Barely said a word."

She regarded him thoughtfully as she chewed. "I understood I was to pretty much keep my mouth shut."

"Keep your..." *Oh, hell.* "Your cousin coached you for your role tonight, I take it."

"Didn't you expect him to?"

"Well..." *Yes.* "I wouldn't have expected him to tell you to 'keep your mouth shut,' for pity's sake."

"He didn't, not in so many words." She broke off another corner of the airy pastry and studied it from different angles. "But the gist of it was, 'Shut up and look good.' Did he have it wrong?" She popped the tidbit into her mouth and drank some more champagne.

No. "It's...well. It's not quite that crudely simple." He hated that she'd made him feel defensive. "It's true that I prefer you to keep a...relatively low profile." At this point, after everything that had transpired, he was downright *desperate* for a date who could put her own agenda on the back burner for one damned night. Why else would he have stooped to going out with arm candy?

"'Keep a low profile'?" she said. "Isn't that just a diplomatic way of saying, 'Shut up and look good'?"

He grimaced and raised his glass to his lips.

"My function tonight is to be every man's fantasy date," she said. "Decorative and acquiescent. I accepted that role, and I've tried to live up to my side of the bargain. Now, to have you call me on the carpet for doing just that..."

"I'm not 'calling you on the carpet,'" he said testily. "I just thought you seemed...almost afraid to speak. I'm not asking you to maintain a vow of silence, after all. You *are* permitted to talk to people!"

"To a point."

Precisely. He expelled a drawn-out sigh. "Are you always this contentious, Miss Armstrong?"

She frowned as she trailed a fingertip through the layer of custard. He knew the "Miss Armstrong" bit nettled her. "I get cranky when I'm tired," she said. "I did try to behave myself in front of the others."

She licked the custard off her finger, the act so offhand, so artless, that for a moment it appeared as if she had no idea how provocative she looked. In fact, the seeming guilelessness of the gesture made it seem all the more potently sensual. David responded on pure instinct, heat pumping through his loins even as his rational mind—conditioned to a high level of suspicion when it came to the motives of the fairer sex—told him it was all a show, it had to be. No woman could be that frankly seductive without being entirely aware of what she was doing.

Sexual allure was Nora Armstrong's stock in trade, David reminded himself. She made her living making love to the camera. How could she not know what she was doing?

Irritation swept in to banish the arousal she'd so swiftly generated. The beguiling sheen of innocence that clung to Nora Armstrong like morning dew was entirely artificial, a studied act calculated to enhance her desirability with the tantalizing lure of the untouched. As bewitching as she was, David found it vexing to be led around by the dick this way, especially since this "date" was supposed to be an arrangement of convenience, devoid of even the whisper of sexual promise.

She was disregarding the ground rules, but why? Was seductiveness simply second nature to her? Was it just that she couldn't help herself, or was there more to it than that?

Did she have, God help him, an agenda?

Gliding another fingertip through the custard, she said, "You know what I think? About you?"

Far more interested than he should have been, David automatically reached for the packet of Dunhills in the inside pocket of his dinner jacket before reminding himself that he couldn't smoke here.

"I think you're a total control freak." She cast him a slightly mischievous glance as she slid her fingertip between her lips.

"Do you?" he said with feigned indifference. Oh, how he hungered for a cigarette. If nothing else, it would give him something to do with his hands, which quivered with the suppressed urge to touch her, something he'd steadfastly avoided all evening.

Seemingly unperturbed by his lack of encouragement, she warmed to her subject while drawing a design in the custard with her finger. "You want everything just so. I shouldn't talk too much, but God forbid I should talk too little. You've got these strict arm candy ground rules I'm supposed to adhere to, but if I try to clarify them, you get all, like—" she adopted a lockjawed send-up of an upper-class English accent "—I say, Miss Armstrong, are you always this bloody contentious?"

He literally bit his lip to keep from smiling. It was bad enough that she wielded the reins of his libido with such practiced ease. Wouldn't do to let her know she had the power to amuse him, as well.

"Harlan claims you're actually a nice guy," she said.

"How extraordinary," he drawled.

"No, I've seen you in action with him. And with the people at this table tonight. You actually *are* nice—considerate, charming, even funny—with everybody but me. Seems that upper lip of yours only gets stiff in my presence."

David choked on his champagne. The body part most affected by Nora Armstrong's presence was located a good deal southward of the upper lip.

Replacing the sheet of pastry on top of the napoleon and dusting off her hands, she said, "I can't help but wonder what it is about me that makes you so uptight. Is it women in general that bug you, or just me? Is there some button of yours I've been pushing without realizing it?"

"I doubt there's anything you do without realizing it, Miss Armstrong."

She stilled, her gaze focusing on him with surprising coolness. "What's that supposed to mean?"

"Absolutely nothing." He sighed with self-disgust for having tumbled so haplessly into this ill-advised little tête-à-tête. Tossing his napkin on the table, he said, "It's late. Shall we call it a night?"

She proceeded to fold her own napkin into a needlessly tidy rectangle. "I was just trying to make conversation."

"If it's clarification of the ground rules you want, may I suggest you refrain from 'making conversation' by dissecting my supposed character flaws?"

Her mouth quirked, and he knew it was because he was coming off like some pompous, self-righteous ass.

All he needed was a monocle and a homburg hat to complete the image.

"*Flaw*," she said. "Singular. Not that you don't have others—I suspect you've got them in abundance—but it was your fixation with control I was making conversation out of."

"And what a riveting subject it was."

She lifted her champagne glass to her mouth. "You could have offered another one."

"You're presupposing a desire for conversation on my part. It's not as if this is an ordinary date, Miss Armstrong. No need to fill the air with pointless chatter."

"You were filling it just as fast as I was." In that mocking English accent, she intoned, "You're yawning again, Miss Armstrong. You're not talking enough, Miss Armstrong. Stop that bloody talking, will you, Miss Armstrong?"

He coughed to cover up the little gust of involuntary laughter that escaped him. "What an uncanny imitation. Correction—*bloody* uncanny."

She chuckled through a yawn. "One of my many hidden talents."

Detouring his thoughts from speculation on the nature of Nora Armstrong's other hidden talents, he pushed back his chair and rose. "You're tired. I'm taking you home."

He pulled her chair out for her and gestured her ahead of him. As they approached the stairs to the main level, he reached out to guide her with a gentlemanly hand on her back, but hesitated. That exquisite gown of hers dipped dramatically in back, the metallic silk settling in waves on the upper slope of a remarkably shapely bottom. Was it really wise to be laying hands on that oh-so-inviting expanse of bare flesh, given the distance he'd striven to establish between them?

Not wise at all, but he did so anyway—he would never see her again after he drove her home; what did it matter?—and found her deliciously sleek and warm to the touch. She tensed slightly as he molded his hand to the small of her back, but she descended the stairs without comment. He let his hand drift down and to the side just a bit, until it met the silken folds of her gown. What he would give to slide his hand beneath those folds, caress that voluptuous bottom, seek out her warm, hidden places, her womanly mysteries....

What would he do if they were the only two people in this ballroom? He imagined sweeping the dishes from a table and throwing her onto it, tearing that flimsy gown from her body and driving himself into her. The fantasy shook him, it was so visceral, so shockingly real.

You sorry wretch. When they reached the main level, David reluctantly shifted his hand to Nora's arm, steering her through the still-crowded ballroom toward the coatroom. *Five months without having it off, and you're ready to ravish a virtual stranger on impulse just because you like the feel of her back against your hand.*

It wasn't that he hadn't had opportunities for sex since he'd broken it off with Helena back in April. He'd dated, after all, even if he'd rarely asked the same woman out twice. Still, he could have bedded any number of those women, if he'd bothered to put out the effort—and if he'd been willing to let himself get snared in yet another doomed liaison, experience having taught him that once he slept with a woman, things tended to spiral out of control. Add to that his inexplicable but fatal attraction to self-serving users, and the very thought of a relationship gave him the sweats.

As David was taking Nora's evening jacket from the sweet-faced young woman acting as coatroom attendant, a man's hand whacked him hard on the back. "David! Where've you been? Mother was asking about you."

David turned to find his rackets partner, Alec Van Aucken, checking out Nora rather too obviously as he withdrew two coat check tickets he'd tucked into his blue velvet cummerbund.

"Alec." David shook his friend's hand. "If I'd known you were going to be here, I'd have looked for you."

"Lying dog!" accused Beryl Van Aucken with an impish smile as she joined them. Alec's widowed mother, one of the doyennes of New York society and an avid philanthropist, resembled a wizened little bird next to her tall, sandy-haired son. In contrast to the haute couture gowns of her peers, she wore a Chinese jacket of scarlet satin with black silk pants. Her snowy hair was twisted into its customary topknot, and around her neck dangled her trademark oversize spectacles on what looked to be a chain of diamantes, although on second thought, they very well might have been diamonds. Beryl loved her diamonds, dozens of which glinted on her fingers and earlobes. With a glance toward Nora, Beryl said, "You were hiding this pretty young thing upstairs where my son couldn't set his sights on her. I don't blame you, knowing Alec."

"You've found me out, Beryl." Leaning down, David kissed her on the cheek with genuine affection. "So good to see you, even if it's just to say goodbye."

"You may be right about him hiding her from me, Mother." Alec accepted a glossy mink coat from the coatroom girl and shook it out. "David usually circulates pretty well at these things, so he must have been deliberately avoiding us—or rather, me. Too intimidated by the competition."

"Where's Patsy tonight, Alec?" David asked pointedly.

"Patsy who?"

"Patsy Crane, your girlfriend."

"Funny. I can't recall having a girlfriend."

"That *is* funny," David said, "considering how many years you've been together."

"As *friends,*" Alec said. "She's like a sister to me."

"It's my fault," Beryl lamented to Nora. "I spoiled him rotten, trying to give him everything I didn't have when I was a kid, and now he's the ultimate Peter Pan. He's got this incredible woman he's been inseparable from since adolescence, a woman who's never shown any interest in any other man, who'd marry him in a second, but he's too busy playing Don Juan to realize what a wonderful thing he's got."

"Far too wonderful to screw up by trying to turn it into something it's not." Alec turned to Nora, unleashing on her his famously charming smile, once described in a *New York* magazine article on eligible bachelors as "winsomely predatory." His voice had an ironed-out uppercrust smoothness, as opposed to that of his mother, who had never completely shed the edgy Brooklyn inflections of her youth. "It would appear," he confided to Nora, "that my greedy friend has been trying to keep you all to himself. You'll notice he hasn't even made introductions yet, and usually he's the last one to fall short when it comes to the social graces."

David groaned inwardly. "Beryl, I'd like you to meet Miss Nora Armstrong. Miss Armstrong, this is Mrs. Beryl Van Aucken. The fellow undressing you with his eyes is her son, Alec."

Nora held her hand out to Alec, who gripped it just a beat too long, and then to Beryl. "I'm pleased to meet you, Mrs. Van Aucken."

"It's Beryl," said the older woman with a smirk in David's direction. "David does have a starchy streak, but *please* tell me he doesn't call you 'Miss Armstrong' in private."

Nora laughed along with Beryl and Alec, as if this were the most preposterous thing she'd ever heard, no doubt reveling in David's grim-faced discomfort. "That would be *seriously* weird."

David pressed his mouth into the shape of a smile and held Nora's jacket open. "Darling, I hate to interrupt all this merriment at my expense, but hadn't we better be—"

"What have we here?" Beryl lifted her gigantic eye-glass to peer at Nora's unorthodox necklace. "Alec, take a look at this."

"I noticed it first thing," replied her son, eyeing the general vicinity of the necklace with an appreciative smile. David shot him a look, to which he responded with an expression of studied innocence. "So I have an eye for pretty baubles."

David glared at him in a way that said, *Look, but don't touch.* Not that he particularly cared whether Alec found her baubles or any other part of her especially riveting, not really. It wasn't as if he had anything emotionally invested in the woman, but there were appearances to maintain. It wouldn't do for David to tolerate another man's open interest in a woman he was ostensibly involved with.

"Interesting," Beryl said, inspecting the necklace—which, given her diminutive stature, was displayed directly in front of her face. "Handmade?"

"Yes."

"It's so intricate. Exquisite, really."

"Thank you!" Nora flashed that devastating smile of hers.

Alec caught David's eye and mouthed, *Nice smile.*

David managed to refrain from clocking him.

"Is the artist someone you know?" Beryl asked Nora.

Nora hesitated, her gaze straying to David briefly before she responded. "Um, yes. Yes. I, uh...it's a friend of mine. Yep." A rosy bloom, for some reason, had suffused her cheeks.

"Does he ever use faceted stones?" Beryl asked. "Something with a little sparkle?"

"She," Nora clarified. "Yes. Absolutely. I have lots of pieces with—that is, lots of *her* pieces with semiprecious faceted stones, and some with both faceted and cabochon."

"You must be one of her best customers, then."

"Um, yeah. Well...I mean, she can always use more. That is, she's always on the lookout for people who appreciate her work and might want to, um..."

"Buy something."

"Yes!"

Beryl lowered her glasses. "Interesting. Not quite my thing—I'm a diamond-and-platinum girl myself. But interesting." Turning to her son, she said, "Alec? Do you have my coat?"

"At your service." While Alec helped his mother into her mink coat, David held the gold brocade jacket open for Nora, who, in an abrupt about-turn, had become strangely subdued.

Alec took his overcoat from the coat check girl and donned it, his gaze never straying from Nora. "I know I've seen you before. Last winter in Aspen, right?"

"Um..."

"At the Caribou Club, maybe?" Alec persisted, ignoring the black look David speared him with as he collected his chesterfield and scarf and dug a tip out of his pocket.

"Um, no, I've never been—"

"The Mandalay, then. I know I saw you last winter. It had to be Aspen."

"I've never been to Aspen."

"I don't see the point of Aspen," Beryl said. "Or Gstaad, for that matter. Why seek out snow in the winter?"

"Mother winters in Palm Beach," Alec told Nora with a little shudder of mock revulsion. "Too many blue-haired ladies in white Bentleys for my taste."

"For mine, too," Beryl conceded, "but at least there I can step outside without zipping myself up in one of those damned space suits they wear in Aspen. Speaking of Palm Beach, my daughters are coming with me this year, and I know they'd love to have some new jewelry to wear there, something different. They both seem to like that sort of thing." She waved a beringed hand toward Nora's necklace. "They're very particular, though. They'd want only certain types of stones, and so forth. Does this friend of yours take commissions?"

"Yes! Oh, definitely. She loves custom work."

"I wish the girls were here tonight, so they could see that on you. They wouldn't want to order anything from your friend without seeing samples of her work."

"Um, well, maybe I could give you my...I mean, I could get their phone numbers," Nora said, unaccountably flustered, "and, um, pass them on to my friend, and she could, you know, set up a meeting to show them some things."

"You don't know my daughters," Beryl said with a roll of her eyes. "They're just as spoiled as Alec, in their own

ways. Neither one of them could be bothered to make an
appointment to look the stuff over, and they wouldn't
keep it even if they did. But if they actually saw the jewelry on you, I know they'd be interested. They'll probably
order a dozen pieces between them. Do you wear it often?"

"It's the only jewelry I ever wear."

"No problem, then. They'll both be at that Museum of
Modern Art jazz thing next week. Wear something really
dazzling and bring your friend's business card."

"Um..." Nora, inexplicably downcast again, looked toward David.

"Don't tell me he hasn't asked you to the MoMA benefit yet." Beryl scowled at David. "I know *you're* going.
It's one of your own events. Ask her to go with you, already. She won't say no. She'll get to help her friend
make a big sale."

David's teeth ached from clenching them. "I'll take it
under advisement."

Alec, his attention still fixed on Nora, snapped his fingers. "St. Bart's, right? All the models winter there. That's
where I saw you—at that insane party at the Saline Beach
villa."

"What makes you so sure I'm a model?" Nora asked.

"A woman as stunning as you?" Alec turned on the
smile. "I'm just surprised I haven't noticed you around
New York before this. Who are you with?"

"With? Oh—uh, Boss."

"Really. I dated a girl last year who'd just signed with
them. She was getting four thousand a day, but I'll bet
you're doing better than that. Those cheekbones alone
are worth an extra grand."

It always astounded David how crass Americans could

be about money, but before he could intervene and drag Nora away, Beryl wrapped her bony little hand around his arm and tugged. "Come with me. I want to talk to you."

3

DAVID ALLOWED HIMSELF to be dragged by this little old mink-coated woman half his size to a quiet corner where they could see Nora and Alec, but not hear them.

Without preamble, Beryl said, "If you're planning on taking someone else to the MoMA thing, cancel out and take Nora instead. She's worth a hundred of those cold-eyed bitches you usually date."

"Cold-eyed..." David chuckled incredulously. "Don't hold back, Beryl—just speak your mind." It was that no-holds-barred candor that most reminded David of his grandmother Sunny. Like Beryl, Sunny had been humbly born, the daughter of a Yorkshire coal miner who'd married above herself but never completely lost the grit under her nails. She'd been the only one in the family who ever took David to task for anything, who ever told it the way it was and blast the consequences. And for that, he'd loved her deeply and wholeheartedly.

Beryl was his Sunny now, the only friend he had in this city—in the world, anymore—who ever looked him in the eye and spoke her mind, a trait that made her both exasperating and indispensible.

"Let me see," Beryl said. "The first cold-eyed bitch had to be that real estate agent, what's-her-name, who brought floor plans for East Side co-ops to that Lincoln Center thing last year and spread them right out on the tables."

"I took her home early and never saw her again." David glanced toward Alec and Nora. He was doing most of the talking, while standing way too close to her; she was stifling a yawn.

"Yeah, she lacked finesse, but that redhead was slicker, the one who'd just made partner at her law firm and was trying to play rainmaker. She used to go through *stacks* of business cards when you weren't looking, and I heard she snared half a dozen deep-pocket clients that way. It took you a little longer to catch on to her."

"Three dates," David said tightly.

"But the worst of the lot was that ice goddess fiancée of yours, that dress designer. Helena something—Parr. Helena Parr."

"We were never officially engaged." But close enough. God, what an ass he'd been, to have been taken in by her, to have thought she actually had feelings for him, when she'd simply been using him to help launch her career in fashion.

"I cringed every time you brought her to one of these charity events," Beryl said. "The second you turned your back, that woman would be working the room like a hooker at an insurance convention. Only it wasn't sex she was selling, it was Helena Parr originals. It worked, too. You can't go to one of these things without seeing at least half a dozen of her idiotic pseudo-Victorian evening gowns with the underwear on the outside. And I hear she's presenting her first big collection in the spring."

"I heard that, too." It wasn't Helena's success that galled him. He wasn't *quite* that petty, and having an erotic appetite for corsets and waist cinchers and such, he actually liked Helena's conceit of sewing them onto the outside of the gowns. The problem was that she'd exploited him to achieve her success, while pretending it was only his company she was interested in. He'd felt like the worst kind of dupe when he'd caught her out, especially given his history with other, equally self-serving women. "I've been a good deal more...discriminating since then." Paranoid was more like it, but better safe than sorry.

"You can't be *that* discriminating," Beryl said. "Alec told me that girl you took to the silent auction last week tried to sell him a sailboat."

"He told me the same thing this morning. I was going to bring her here tonight, but I canceled."

"Good. You're better off with Nora. She seems very real, very genuine. There's a frankness about her, a sweetness."

You haven't seen her eat a napoleon, David thought. Across the room, Alec was casually touching Nora's arm as he expounded on whatever it was he was expounding on. David's hands, which he'd shoved in his coat pockets, tightened into fists.

"She's arm candy, isn't she?" Beryl asked.

David stared at the old woman as her knowing smile grew smug.

"I knew it," she said. "Left to your own devices, you'll pick Cruella De Vil every time. Since Nora is pretty much the Anticruella, it stands to reason that somebody else must have picked her for you."

David slid a hand into the pocket that held his cigarettes, swore under his breath and withdrew it. It was true; his taste in women had plummeted dramatically somewhere along the way. He hadn't always been such a sucker for wicked witches.

"My only question," Beryl said, "is why you don't just go to these things stag? It'd be a lot less complicated."

"More so, actually. I'd be viewed as *available* then.

Sooner or later I'd get sucked into another relationship, and I've sworn off them."

"For good? Won't that be kind of lonely?"

"Better to be alone than to get so used to playing the fool that I actually become one." With another glance toward Alec and Nora, David asked, "Do you think he knows?"

"That she's arm candy? Nah, he's as dumb as a post when it comes to beautiful women, takes them entirely at face value."

"You won't tell him, will you?"

"God, no. If he knew she was up for grabs, he'd waste no time dragging her off to the nearest cave, which would be just one more roadblock in the way of getting him together with Patsy. Did you know he gave her a ring last week?"

"Not an engagement ring, surely."

"He calls it a friendship ring." She rolled her eyes. "A sapphire the size of your fist, but it's just a 'token of friendship.'" She shook her head disgustedly. "How did I manage to raise such an dimwit? He won't even sleep with that poor girl, and I suspect she's saving herself for him. Meanwhile, he's running around with every silicone-enhanced glamourpuss in New York. Would you talk to him for me?"

"I have. He says Patsy doesn't interest him sexually. I gather that tasteful old-money image of hers just doesn't turn him on."

"Is that it? He needs thigh-high skirts and push-up bras? Now I know what to get Patsy for her birthday."

"Do you never tire of meddling in other people's lives, Beryl?"

"It beats raising orchids. Anyway, don't worry about

Alec finding out your new girlfriend is arm candy. You'll have her all to yourself."

"What makes you think I want her?"

"I see the way you're looking at her."

He grimaced. "It's not like that, Beryl. This is strictly an arrangement. She's nobody, just a model."

"That girl's not *just* anything. There's something about her, David."

"Please don't tell me again how sweet she is." He wasn't quite as gullible as Alec when it came to beautiful women.

"It's not just that," Beryl said. "She has...character. There are layers to her, hidden depths. You don't see it?"

He sighed heavily. "She was *supposed* to be uncomplicated."

"Whoever told you that," Beryl chuckled, "is guilty of false advertising."

TUCKED INTO THE PASSENGER seat of David Waite's Jag as he drove her home on darkened, near-empty streets, Nora closed her eyes—which she was having an awfully hard time keeping open, given the complete absence of conversation—and mentally debriefed herself.

All in all, she had to give her performance this evening no better than a C. She'd started out pretty well, playing the grinning, zip-lipped arm candy role to perfection, but it had been a trying performance, and as the evening wore on and fatigue crept up on her, she'd gradually metamorphosed from bimbo to shrew.

She shouldn't have yammered on about how she was expected to "shut up and look good." She definitely shouldn't have badgered him about his stupid arm candy ground rules. And where, exactly, had her head been when she'd asked, "You know what I think? About you?"

Are you always this contentious, Miss Armstrong? Yikes, had she totally blown it? Harlan would not be pleased if this ended up reflecting badly on him. He'd counted on her to live up to her end of the bargain. He'd coached her and pleaded with her, and she'd let him down.

After everything he'd done for her, asking so little in return, she'd let him down.

Please, God, don't let David Waite be so royally pissed at me that he takes it out on Harlan. Please, please, please...

And not only had she let Harlan down, she'd blown it for herself, sabotaging a precious opportunity to cultivate the patronage of Beryl Van Aucken's daughters. *They'll probably order a dozen pieces between them,* Beryl had said. It could have been just the boost, both in terms of income and exposure, that Nora's fledgling jewelry business needed. It could have put her on the map. But she'd never find out, because at this point, David loathed her too much to even think about inviting her to that MoMA benefit.

"Are you asleep?"

Nora popped her eyes open and sat up. "No."

David braked at a red light without looking at her, his shadowy profile a study in harsh edges—the slightly prominent brow, the high-bridged Roman nose, the jaw that jutted just a tad too far out, like that of a creature bred to shred meat from bones.

He was an enigma, this semihostile Englishman with his brooding good looks and air of mystery. She knew nothing about him except that he'd studied law at Oxford, and she only knew that because Harlan had told her. During the four hours they'd just spent together, David Waite had volunteered absolutely no personal revelations, nor had he asked her the first thing about herself.

He intimidated her. He'd intimidated her all evening, consciously, it seemed. She hated that feeling of being cowed by somebody. Maybe it hadn't just been exhaustion making her petulant. Maybe it had also been a reaction to the subtle undercurrent of animosity that he wore around him like armor. Negative vibes tended to be contagious.

"Mind if I smoke?" he asked, reaching beneath his coat and producing a box labeled Dunhill.

"Do you want the truth or polite consent?" *Shut up. Shut up! Why can't you just shut up?*

At least that got him to look at her. "Polite consent, of course."

"Go ahead, then," she said through a yawn. "I'd mind more if this were a real date. Men who smoke are not exactly catches."

A hint of a grimace crossed his features as he returned the cigarettes to their pocket. The light turned green and he drove on. "Do spare me the lecture on cancer and heart disease."

"And emphysema."

"Why did I think you might spare me?"

"And sexual dysfunction." *Shut up! SHUT UP!*

"I beg your pardon?"

"Smoking causes impotence. I saw it on 'Sixty Minutes'."

"Rubbish."

"No, it's true. It reduces the blood supply to the, um..."

"Thank you, I get the picture." A smattering of raindrops struck the windshield; David flicked on the wipers with an impatient gesture.

"And talk about bad breath." She made a face. "I kissed a smoker once. I'll never do it again."

"Feel free to close your eyes and nod off again anytime the spirit moves you."

"I think I'm getting my second wind."

"Is that a threat?" The rain started falling harder; David switched the wipers from intermittent to steady.

"Why are you so afraid to have a conversation with me?" she asked.

"I'm not afraid of it," he said, "but I do find it a bit tedious, given your quarrelsome nature...."

"That's only because I'm tired," she interjected.

"And, to be perfectly frank, I really don't see the point. You said it yourself—this is not a real date. We've no obligation to entertain each other, or impress each other, or whatever else it is people on dates are trying to accomplish when they chat each other up ad nauseam. There's something to be said for silence, and right now, if it's all the same to you, I'd appreciate a little of it."

"You have got to be *the* Lord High Control Freak of the Universe," she said. "A total obsessive dominator."

"Ten minutes," he said wearily. "Just until I get you home, and then you'll never have to deal with me or my nasty obsessive domination ever again. Think you can manage that?"

She drew an imaginary zipper across her mouth and snuggled down in the passenger seat. When she breathed deeply, she could detect a lingering hint of new-car smell, which Harlan had once described as "the most potent aphrodisiac known to man or woman."

Nora had never ridden in a Jag before—or in any high-end sports car, for that matter. She'd almost mentioned that earlier in the evening, when she'd first seen the sleek black two-seater parked on the street in front of Harlan's building, but had thought better of it. David Waite would assume that a woman like her—a globe-trotting, champagne-swilling, high-fashion model—was used to being transported in style.

Her gaze drifted to his hands, illuminated at intervals as they passed under street lamps—the left guiding the leather-and-wood steering wheel with economical movements, the right curled lightly around the gearshift's walnut knob. They really were beautiful hands, strong and capable, but at the same time strangely elegant.

Gradually her eyes drifted closed, the pattering of the rain, the *shush, shush, shush* of the wipers and the vibrations of the road making her feel not so much sleepy as entranced, mesmerized. An image coalesced in her mind of David Waite's hands caressing a woman's smooth flesh, rhythmic and coaxing, and try as she might, she couldn't dismiss it. She imagined the trail of warmth those hands would leave in their wake, the heat they'd ignite, the sighs and whimpers.

These were the hands of a man who knew how to touch a woman, who liked touching women, who knew all the places to stroke and explore, and all the ways to do it....

DAVID STARED straight ahead as he drove through the worsening rain, alternately grateful and disappointed to have finally bullied Nora Armstrong into silence.

And it had been bullying, no two ways about it. Having been brought up to pamper women, to treat them with every respect and see to their every need, it sat poorly with him to have browbeaten her that way, regardless that she'd goaded him into it.

"Miss Armstrong," he began, focusing on the rain-slicked road in front of him so he wouldn't have to look her in the eye while he owned up to her low opinion of him. "I know you think I'm something of a bastard. I don't blame you. I just want you to know..."

He shook his head in frustration. "You should know it's not you, not really. You didn't do such a bad job of it tonight, and I didn't mean to come off as such a...well, I mean, I did, I suppose. But I just wanted you to know it's not you. It's me. And...issues that have nothing to do with you. I know you don't want my life story, and God knows I've no desire to share it, but..."

He shrugged. "For what it's worth, if I've made you completely miserable tonight, I want you to know I'm..."

At least look at her while you say this bit. He turned toward her, his pitifully cack-handed apology fading in his throat when he saw her.

She was asleep.

Oh, hell, he thought, realizing she hadn't heard a word he'd said, and then, *What does it matter, anyway?* He'd never see her again after tonight. Why embarrass them both with an unseemly display of penitence? She'd probably only laugh at him later; perhaps she and Harlan and Harlan's boyfriend, whose name David couldn't recall, would all get a good chuckle out of it.

This arm candy bit was supposed to keep things simple, manageable. Why, then, did he feel an inexorable unraveling of his carefully laid plans, a slow erosion of his mastery over the situation? It was almost as bad as a bona fide relationship.

Almost.

He turned onto Harlan's street, pulled the car up in front of his building, cut the engine and cleared his throat. "Miss Armstrong."

She didn't move, curled down in the seat with her

head tilted to the side, her mouth slightly open and her hands resting limply, palms up, on her lap.

"Miss Armstrong. We're here."

Nothing, not the slightest flutter of an eyelash. Light from a street lamp filtered through the rain-dappled windshield, washing her in a silvery radiance that danced and quivered like something alive. Golden tendrils of her hair had come loose to drape sinuously over her shoulders and chest.

Her jacket had fallen open, revealing luxuriant breasts stretching the whisper of silk that covered them. Extraordinarily beautiful, infused with the vibrancy of youth and bathed in watery luminescence, Nora Armstrong looked for all the world like a wood nymph found sleeping in some secret grotto.

A wood nymph, David? A wood nymph, *for pity's sake? Do get a grip.* Taking his Dunhills and his lighter out of his pocket, David rolled his window down halfway. It rained in on him a bit, but not too badly. He lit a cigarette and breathed gratefully of the fragrant smoke, blowing it out the window.

Smoking causes impotence. I saw it on "Sixty Minutes."

"Bloody hell." David flung the cigarette out into the rain, rolled the window up and turned once more toward his dozing passenger. "Miss Armstrong."

No response.

He reached toward her, hesitated, then lightly stroked her cheek; it felt hot against his fingertips. "Miss Armstrong," he said more softly. "Wake up. We're here."

She squirmed sleepily, raised one hand to swat at her cheek where he'd touched it, then settled back down, as if intending to spend the rest of the night there.

Leaning over her, he gathered her disorderly hair be-

All of Me

hind her ear and trailed the back of his hand down her face. A little louder, he said, "Time to wake up."

Her eyes opened, and only then did he realize how close he was to her, mere inches away. Clearly startled, she gasped at his nearness, flinched at his touch.

He backed away. "You fell asleep. We're here."

She looked around dazedly. "Where?"

"Your cousin's place in Chelsea."

It took her a moment, and then recognition set in. "Oh." She slumped back in her seat and rubbed her eyes. "I thought I was still on the train," she said thickly.

"What train?"

"The train from Cleve—" She opened her eyes, glanced at him. "Tahiti," she said, then let out a sleepy little giggle. "The train from Tahiti."

"There are no trains from Tahiti."

"Dreams are like that." Nora leaned back in her seat and stretched, eyes closed, her body shivering deliciously.

David imagined her writhing like that beneath him, naked and warm, and felt a surge of lust that took his breath away. "Right. Uh...listen, gather yourself together and I'll walk you to the door."

"You don't have to do that."

"Of course I do. It's after midnight, and I don't like the looks of this neighborhood. It wasn't that long ago they were calling it Hell's Kitchen."

"If you insist. Thanks." As she bent over to retrieve her bag, which lay on the floor at her feet, her hair came tumbling loose from what remained of its chignon, both feathered picks slipping free. David caught one as it fell and handed it to her; she tucked it in her purse and felt around for the other.

He snapped on the courtesy light and tried to help her

look, but the little ornament seemed to have vaporized into thin air. The satin waves of her hair swayed as she moved, emitting the sweetly evocative fragrance of lavender.

He leaned toward her side of the car, groping around the seat and gearshift, her hair sweeping against his face, lightly, teasingly, her hands brushing his and then quickly withdrawing. The effect of all that tentative touching, her nearness, her scent, was damn near maddening.

He reached up and flipped off the light. "I'll find it tomorrow and get it back to you. It's late. Let's get you inside."

She looked up at him with those huge, insightful eyes of hers, and he knew she felt it, too, the crackle of awareness, the tug of desire. Surely she must feel it, he thought, his gaze on her mouth. She did feel it. She couldn't simply be toying with him.

And neither could Helena—or the others. And yet they had.

He drew away, yanked on the door handle. She started to open her door, too, but he said, "No, wait there. I'll come round."

He stepped out into the rain, divesting himself of his chesterfield as he circled the car. Opening her door, he reached for her hand to help her out, holding the coat over her to shield her from the rain. They sprinted to the front door, but it took Nora a bit of fumbling with the keys to figure out which one opened it.

Stepping inside, she handed him his coat. "Thank you," she said with a finality that indicated she expected him to leave now.

"I'm going upstairs with you."

She blinked at him.

"When I said I was walking you to your door," he explained as he got back into his now dripping coat, "I meant to your apartment door. This isn't exactly a secure building. Anybody could be prowling these hallways."

She allowed him to escort her upstairs in that antiquated old death trap of a lift, and into the dismal little sixth floor vestibule. After trying key after key in the door's several locks, she finally got it open. Turning to face him, she said, "Thank you again."

"Thank *you*," he said, "for accommodating me on such short notice."

Even under the merciless glare of that single overhead lightbulb, with her hair untidy and her eye makeup slightly smudged, she stole the very breath from his lungs. Her eyes were more languorous than ever from her nap in the car, her cheeks blood flushed, her lips, now devoid of lipstick, a deep, all-too-kissable pink. His gaze traveled downward, lighting on the amber pendant snugged between her breasts, and the dark spot within it, which he still hadn't gotten a good look at.

"Indulge me." From his coat pocket, he produced his reading spectacles—half glasses, actually—and slid them on. When he raised a hand to her chest, she grew very still, watching him intently as he lifted the chunk of amber, cradling it in his palm. It felt good there, smooth and surprisingly light, but not as good as Nora's soft flesh against the back of his hand.

It *was* an insect, he saw, but a rather remarkable one, intact and beautifully formed. With its lacy wings and long antennae, it somewhat resembled a mayfly.

He turned the nugget over in his hand to view the insect from different angles, his knuckles grazing the resilient warmth of her breasts as he did so. It was a stolen caress, almost but not completely inadvertent, and totally beyond his power to resist.

Five months is definitely too long to go without touching a woman, he thought as he savored the moment.

Her breathing quickened. He sensed the rapid rise and fall of her breasts against his hand and was gratified that she felt at least something in response to his touch—unless it was just indignation.

"It's rather sad, really," he said with a nod toward the little creature who'd lighted on the wrong tree trunk a million years ago and ended up buried in its resin for all eternity. "Poor fellow never had a chance."

"Look at it this way," she said. "He's achieved a sort of splendor in death that he never had in life. In a way, he's become immortal. Not such a terrible fate for a bug."

"I suppose some traps are more alluring than others." David allowed his fingers to stroke her softly as he released the pendant. "But they are, after all, still traps."

He removed his spectacles and stowed them back in their pocket. When he looked up, he found her studying him with an almost melancholy expression, as if wondering what had made him so bitter.

"Good night, Miss Armstrong." He turned and left.

4

"MRS. VAN AUCKEN on line one," announced David's secretary over the intercom, the clipped efficiency of her tone ameliorated somewhat by that mellifluous Jamaican accent.

"Thank you, Mrs. Watley." David lifted the receiver and punched the button for line one with the butt end of his fountain pen. "Good morning, Beryl. To what do I owe—"

"Did you ask her yet?"

"Did I ask who what?"

There came a staticky sigh. "Did you ask Nora Armstrong to the MoMA benefit? It's tomorrow night. Don't tell me you didn't ask her."

"I never said I would." Reaching across his carved oak desk, a ponderous old Victorian piece, like everything else in his office, he returned the pen to the antique jam jar that held his writing implements—and which, for the past six days, had also been home to a certain jeweled and feathered hair pick, which he intended someday, when he tired of looking at it, to return to its proper owner.

"You're a moron, David."

"Pursuing a relationship with Miss Armstrong would make me a moron, Beryl." Resisting the urge to pluck the hair pick out of the jar and fiddle with it—a newfound nervous habit—David leaned back in his tufted leather chair, loosened his tie and opened his top shirt button.

"You *do* call her Miss Armstrong!" she cackled. "What a tight-ass! I'll bet you iron your boxer shorts, too."

"Very funny." He *had* them ironed.

"Ask her to the MoMA thing," Beryl commanded. "Or did you already ask someone else?"

"Actually, I was thinking I might give the whole thing a miss."

"You mean, not go? I can't think the museum trustees would be very amused if you just blew off such an important event—especially when you're the one who talked them into it."

"Neither can I," he sighed.

"So, call Nora."

"Our date last week was intended as strictly a one-time deal, and I'm quite sure there was little pleasure in it for her." His fault entirely, of course, but no sense going into all that. "Trust me, she'd be just as happy never to see me again."

Beryl snorted with laugher. "God, you *are* dense. And blind as a bat. Remember the way you were looking at her the other night?"

Yes. "No."

"Well, she was looking at you the same way."

"If that's so, how can I have failed to notice it?"

"Because you are a *dense, blind moron,*" the widow explained helpfully.

"It's been great chatting with you, Beryl, but now I really must be—"

"Don't be a *putz*, David. Call her."

"She'll hang up on me. By now, I'm just an irritating memory to her. More likely, she's put me completely out of her mind."

"Just like you've put her completely out of your mind?" Beryl asked slyly.

Touché. She'd haunted his thoughts all week. David rummaged through the papers on his desk for his packet of Dunhills and lit one.

"You should give those things up," Beryl said as the cigarette ignited. Her hearing was *way* too acute for a woman her age. "Now they're saying they cause impotence. It was on 'Sixty Minutes.'"

God help me.

"Get that patch thing," she suggested.

"I'll take it under advisement," he said, sucking defiantly on his cigarette.

"Yeah, that's your way of telling me to take a flying—"

"What's that, Mrs. Watley?" David said loudly. "Another call on line two? Who? No, no, quite right. Mustn't keep His Eminence waiting."

"Nice try, David. Now, listen up. I want Nora Armstrong to go to that MoMA benefit tomorrow night. And maybe to that Tavern on the Green Kidney Foundation thing next week. Oh, and there's that fashion show for breast cancer awareness the week after that."

"She's arm candy, Beryl, not a steady girlfriend."

"That could change. I like her. You like her—more than you probably even realize, given what a dim bulb you can be. Look, you've got to at least take her to the MoMA thing tomorrow. I talked up that jewelry to my daughters, and they're looking forward to her being there."

"So is Alec, no doubt." David tapped his cigarette a bit too forcefully into the giant alabaster ashtray on his desk.

"Patsy Crane's going, which means Alec will be on his good behavior."

"I didn't know he knew any good behavior. Look,

Beryl, I know you don't really care whether your daughters get to order jewelry from Nora Armstrong's friend. You've got this notion there's some grand romance waiting to be played out between us. Quite wrong, I promise you, and even if it were true—*especially* if it were true—I'd steer well clear of the woman. The last thing I'm in the market for right now is some torturous love affair."

"Love affairs are only torturous if you choose partners who know how to turn the screws, which, of course, is your forte. But since someone of remarkably better judgment chose Nora for you, you should give her a fair shake before throwing her back, don't you think?"

"No, I don't. Beryl, I know you mean well, but it's just not in the cards. I'm not about to court disaster by getting entangled in a relationship with Nora Armstrong or anyone else. Thank you for caring enough to make such a tiresome pest of yourself, but the answer is no. I'm not going to ask her to the MoMA benefit."

"You think I'm gonna give up just like that?" Beryl challenged. "Who, exactly, do you think you're dealing with, David? I'm the daughter of a Brooklyn numbers runner, not one of these spineless old-money hothouse flowers bred to be a good sport in the face of defeat. Not only do I not lose with grace, I *don't lose.*"

David grinned indulgently as he blew a stream of smoke across his office. "Are you telling me you always get your own way? One hundred percent of the time?"

"David, I'm a million years old, I've got more money than Trump and I've made damn sure everybody I know owes me at least one favor. You, for instance, owe me somewhere in the neighborhood of half a million by now."

"Ah."

"Ah, indeed. Those fat checks I write you at the drop of a hat could dry right up."

"You wouldn't do that." Besides being his friend, Beryl was one of a handful of private benefactors who could always be counted on to donate generously in cases of acute need—earthquakes in South America, famine in Africa, hurricanes, floods, fires, epidemics...it seemed there was always a life-threatening disaster somewhere. What with David's fund-raising expertise and contacts, he was in an ideal position to tap people like Beryl for the quick infusions of cash needed to bring these crises under control—sans commission, of course. It was strictly pro bono work.

"Oh, wouldn't I?" she asked. "My checkbook has always been open for you, David. You want it, you got it. But I ask you to do one little thing—"

"I can't believe you'd be so craven as to withhold money from such desperately needy—"

"You've got other donors. You don't need me."

"Beryl, you *know* you're the only one who never grills me about what it's for, never makes me wait or submit tedious paperwork."

"I spoiled you. It's a bad habit of mine, indulging the people I care about. Well, no more. The well's run dry, David. Live with it."

David grimaced and put out his cigarette. "I give in, Beryl. I'll take Miss Armstrong to the MoMA benefit. *If* she'll go with me."

Beryl whooped in victory. "And the Tavern on the Green? And the fashion show?"

"I'll take it under—"

"I feel that checkbook snapping shut."

He bit out the sort of swear word he normally never uttered in the presence of women. "You win, Beryl. Happy?"

"Deliriously. You won't regret this, David."

"I already do."

After bidding her goodbye, David dropped the receiver none too gently into its cradle, rested his elbows on the desk and scrubbed his hands over his face, muttering a stream of ripe expletives.

He uncovered his face, his gaze homing in on the flamboyant little hair pick snuggled up incongruously amongst the antique fountain pens and mechanical pencils in the jam jar. With a sigh of surrender, he reached across and snatched it out, then settled back and held it in front of his face, turning it this way and that.

The pick itself, rather than being a simple shaft, like a chopstick, had been fashioned of brass to resemble a slightly bent little tree twig, complete with tiny buds. The business end was pointed, the top end crowned with a cluster of semiprecious stones and a jaunty little tuft of feathers. It was obviously handmade, probably by the same person who made Nora's jewelry.

There was something about the rustic elegance of this common little twig all dressed up in jewels and feathers that reminded him of Nora. It should have looked tawdry, even silly, but somehow it didn't. There was a balance to it, a rightness, that appealed to him.

He held the feathers to his nose and breathed in the scent that clung to them from having been in contact with her hair, an achingly familiar scent, the perfume of his boyhood in the English countryside—lavender. His maiden aunt Enid's garden path had been edged with great masses of it, and its fragrance had always struck him as being exceptionally soft and unworldly, just like her.

It was the perfect scent for Nora, he thought, only to chide himself for his naïveté. There was nothing un-worldly about Nora Armstrong, not really. The ingenue aura was a façade, meant to enhance her sexual appeal. It was all very calculated, very well thought out. And beau-tifully acted, worthy of an Academy Award.

Had he really just agreed to take her out three more times? He flung the pick onto his desk and raked both hands through his hair.

His carefully laid plans weren't just unraveling, they were exploding. The whole idea of dating arm candy was to avoid any sort of personal relationship with a woman. That was enough of a challenge, given that Nora Arm-strong—part ingenue, part seductress—had captured him so effortlessly in her sexual thrall.

It was like some Noel Coward farce with David play-ing the anal-retentive git whose efforts to avoid romantic involvement are mere fodder for the whims of fate. Yet, girding his loins, he rises to the challenge, not only resist-ing temptation but alienating the ingenue so thoroughly that she couldn't possibly want anything more to do with him. *Well done!* he exclaims as the curtain closes on Act One.

Act Two: Enter, from stage left, Lady Beryl Van Aucken, who thinks it would be a bit of a lark to play matchmaker. As the git is heavily indebted to her, it's lit-tle trouble to blackmail him into escorting the ingenue around town in the hope of complicating the plot with a laborious little romance sure to generate plenty of laugh-ter at the git's expense.

As things stood now, David was in real danger of trad-ing in his title of Lord High Control Freak of the Universe for that of Hapless Buffoon. He loathed that feeling of be-ing buffeted about by circumstances beyond his control, especially when those circumstances were conspiring to thrust him into yet another unwanted relationship.

A relationship which, in fact, already existed—or soon would—if one defined a relationship as more than one date. The trick was to keep that relationship purely impersonal, purely business. To do that, he would need to seize the reins and hold them in an iron fist, regardless of Nora's or Beryl's or anyone else's agenda.

If there was to be an Act Three, he would damn well be the one to write it.

He stabbed his intercom button. "Mrs. Watley, get through to Harlan Armstrong, would you? You'll find his number in my business card file. Er...his cell phone, not his apartment." David didn't want Nora answering the phone. For one thing, she very well might hang up on him. For another, it was far better to use Harlan as an intermediary in setting up these dates. Made the whole business more...*businesslike.*

"I've got Mr. Armstrong on line one, Mr. Waite."

"Thank you." David lifted the phone and pressed line one. "Good morning, Harlan."

"David! How's it goin'?" Street sounds provided a muted backdrop to Harlan's voice. "I've been meaning to call you with some ideas I had for events you might want to think about, but I was gonna wait till after I got back from the islands. We fly out tomorrow morning, me and Kevin, and we'll be back on the twenty-fifth. Two weeks of suntan oil and pig roasts."

"Sounds..." *Greasy.* "...Delightful."

"So, how did it go last week with Nora at the Red Cross thing?"

"Surely she's given you a full accounting."

"Nah, I can't get much from her. She's been so tight-lipped that I've been...you know, kind of worried that it didn't go real well. That's really why I haven't called before now."

"Actually, she's the reason I'm calling. I've set up a thousand-dollar-a-ticket evening of jazz at the Museum of Modern Art to benefit their expansion project. It's tomorrow night, and I was wondering if, ah...if your cousin would be interested in going. Strictly the same arrangement as before," he added quickly.

"The arm candy thing."

"Right. In fact, it occurred to me she might consider making it sort of a regular thing—you know, at least for awhile."

"A regular thing," Harlan said. "Like a...steady girl-friend?"

"I suppose it would look to outsiders as if we were going about together. But of course, between the two of us it would simply be..."

Harlan waited him out.

"You know. An arm candy thing, as you said." David fumbled for his cigarettes and lit one. "Do you think she'd be interested?"

"I don't know, David. She thought it was gonna be just a one-shot deal, you know?"

"Well, do you think you could talk her into it?"

"Possibly." There came a moment of dead air, and then Harlan said, "You know, I was just thinking, there's no reason we can't meet today to discuss those ideas of mine. No need to wait till I come back from vacation. Are you free for lunch? I know you're probably a 21 Club kind of guy, but there's this great new sushi bar on Fiftieth between Sixth and Seventh—Nishino."

So that's how it's to be. David bought a moment of deliberation by taking a lingering drag of his cigarette. Harlan was evidently willing to ask Nora to extend her arm candy stint, but only if David let him pitch ideas over raw fish and rice wine.

"I assume you eat sushi," Harlan persisted. "Somebody told me you lived in Japan once."

This had been Harlan's agenda all along, David realized. By bailing him out with arm candy, he'd hoped to ingratiate himself with David so that David would hire him to plan an event. Nothing particularly untoward in that on the surface, although it galled him to be manipulated by yet another actor in this little farce, the plot of which grew more convoluted with every scene that was played out.

"My treat," Harlan prodded.

How badly did David need Beryl's money? Not that badly. There were other zillionaires in the sea.

His gaze lit on the hair pick lying atop a mound of papers on his desk. Stubbing out his half-smoked cigarette, he picked it up and twirled it slowly, brought it to his mouth and brushed the feathers lightly across his lips.

"David...?"

"I'll be there at noon." David hung up as Harlan was saying goodbye.

5

"I APPRECIATE YOUR DOING this for me, Miss Armstrong,"
said David Waite to the windshield as he guided his Jag
through the twilit streets of Manhattan toward the Museum of Modern Art.

So it's still "Miss Armstrong." The archaic formality,
which Nora had welcomed at first, had swiftly worn thin.
"You can call me Nora, you know. I mean, this *is* our second date."

"Our second simulated date," he said without so much
as a glance in her direction. "If it's all the same to you, I'd
rather call you Miss Armstrong."

The subtext of which was, of course, *Kindly do not pre-
sume to call me David.*

Nora couldn't keep her eyebrows from quirking.
"Okaaay..."

He must have struck even himself as cold, because he
added, in a gentler tone, "Best to keep things on an impersonal footing. I'm sure you agree."

She shrugged negligently. "No skin off my nose, Mr.
Waite." Some impish whim made her add, "It is *Mr.*
Waite, I assume—not *Lord* Waite, or maybe Your Excel-
lency?"

He didn't smile, but his eyes did flick in her direction,
with a slight snap to them that, in another man, might almost have been mistaken for amusement. His gaze swept
over her, a fleeting and seemingly appreciative appraisal

of her scoop-necked, sleeveless, stretch lace cocktail dress, one of half a dozen Kevin had chosen and altered for her before leaving for the airport that morning. She wore her hair in a French twist secured with about two dozen pins, which had taken her a good forty-five minutes to do. On her feet were the requisite spine-bending stiletto heels, in burnished silver to match her clutch purse and leather bolero jacket.

But her most important accessory was, of course, her jewelry, since she would essentially be modeling it to-night for Beryl Van Aucken's daughters. She'd chosen her newest pieces, which she'd crafted during the past week—necklace, ring, bracelets and earrings in the form of intricate webs of silver vines encrusted with tiny fresh-water pearls and quartz crystals.

David was dressed as he had been a week ago, in stan-dard-issue black tie and that black topcoat with the white silk scarf draped carelessly over his shoulders. Most of the men at last week's event had gussied up their ensem-bles with colorful cummerbunds and vests, but not Da-vid Waite. There was an almost austere quality to his at-tire, like that of a priest's habit: classic black dinner suit and bow tie, plain white silk shirt, black patent shoes. The only variation from last week was that tonight his shirt studs appeared to be onyx; last week they'd been mother-of-pearl.

Returning his attention to the road, David said, "You seem cross again. I thought you only got that way when you were tired. Out carousing till dawn again last night, were you?"

"I happen to be perfectly well rested," she said with feigned good humor. "I'm not cross at all, just poking a little fun. In our country, it's called *humor*."

He stared grimly ahead, but his mouth twitched, infinitesimally. Was she actually getting to him?

Did she want to?

Or, more to the point, *should* she want to?

She cleared her throat. "Look, no offense, Mr. Waite, but much as I appreciate your thanking me for doing this, I assume you know I'm not really doing it for you."

"I do know that. You're doing it for your cousin. I extracted the truth from him at lunch yesterday, all about how you agreed to the arm candy bit because you think you owe it to him. He didn't go into the particulars, but I gather you feel significantly indebted to him."

"I owe him big-time," she said. "He's also my favorite cousin—my favorite *person*, if you want to know the truth. I'd do anything for Harlan. Anything at all."

"Even tolerate my rather disagreeable company on a semiregular basis?"

"Yes."

A muscle pulsed on the side of David's jaw. "Spoken like a woman who just realized she's made a deal with the devil. Having second thoughts?"

"If you mean am I gonna try and get out of it, no. A deal is a deal."

"Your sacrifice is commendable. And has already, in fact, borne fruit for your cousin. Harlan ran a few ideas past me during our lunch, ideas for attracting young donors. I thought he had a tile loose at first—your cousin has some rather strange notions of how to throw a party—but a couple of his proposals actually have some merit. We're going ahead with one of them after he gets back from the islands."

"The *Little Exes* thing. He told me."

Harlan had returned from his lunch with David yesterday buzzing with excitement. He'd suggested a benefit performance of Kevin's rock musical, *Two Little Exes*, followed by a party in the lobby of its Chelsea theater, Pandora's Box, where the audience could meet the cast, with all proceeds going to AIDS research. David gave him the go-ahead and the producers okayed it via a phone call from the restaurant, during which it was penciled in for October 16, five weeks from now. If it went well, David would probably okay a more ambitious out-of-town event Harlan had in mind for Halloween night.

There was just one catch, Harlan had sheepishly explained. He'd kind of promised to persuade Nora into an open-ended gig as David Waite's semiconstant companion. Once Nora had recovered from her astonishment that David would want to have anything more to do with her, given what a pain in the butt she'd been, she reflected on the two big advantages and one big disadvantage of turning her isolated guest appearance into a continuing role.

The first advantage was, of course, the benefit to Harlan's career, a you-scratch-my-back arrangement that David was aware of and evidently complicit in. No problem.

A bit trickier was the benefit to Nora's career—the potential for jewelry commissions from the Van Aucken daughters and possibly others—of which David must remain entirely unaware, lest he realize that she and Harlan had been misleading him from the beginning about her being a model.

She'd tried to circumvent that problem altogether by pleading with Harlan that they had to fess up to David right away, before things went any further, about her true vocation, but Harlan wouldn't hear of it. Far from appreciating the truth, he'd maintained, David would be incensed that they'd lied to him at all. He would refuse to have anything more to do with either one of them, which would stymie his career and prevent hers from getting the jump start it otherwise might have.

It's business, Harlan had told her when she'd bemoaned having to live a lie whenever she was with David Waite. *Everybody lies in business.*

And that, of course, was the one big disadvantage of the arrangement—Nora's having to deceive David Waite on an ongoing basis about who she was and what she did for a living. It made her queasy to engage in such subterfuge—but it made her queasier to think of having to leave New York City, which she was already growing to love, and crawl back to Ohio and her job in that rib joint because she couldn't get her jewelry business off the ground. This arm candy stint was a golden opportunity for a farm-bred Midwestern girl to make contacts in New York, and after she'd thought it all through, she found that she couldn't pass it up. It remained to be seen how she would manage to take and fill jewelry orders without blowing her cover, but if she just kept her wits about her, that would likely sort itself out.

The final factor in her ruminations, which she had yet to categorize as either an advantage or a disadvantage, was David Waite himself. Or rather, her reaction to him, which she'd be hard-pressed to define. He was exasperating, yes—surly, distant, even downright insulting—with her alone. What did that mean? And what did it mean that she'd found herself obsessing about him all week, like a teenybopper with her latest crush?

She replayed their conversations in her mind ad infinitum, recalling the soft rumble of his voice and how it seemed to resonate right through her skin. Recalling the dark intensity of his gaze. Twice he'd found excuses to put his hands on her and let them linger there, hot and rough; both times the raw, startling pleasure of it had just about stopped her heart. Nora had been touched by men before—she'd gone as far as light petting—but never had she felt this visceral reaction to it. Never had it made her dizzy and weak in the knees, which she'd always thought were clichés.

Never had it made her want more.

She stole a glance at David—diabolically handsome, fiercely aloof...and a complete enigma. Maybe that was part of his appeal, the fact that she knew so little about him. Would it help to burst the bubble of infatuation that enveloped her if she could strip away some of that aura of mystery he'd shrouded himself in?

"So," she began, "Harlan tells me you have a law degree from Oxford."

"Then he's been misinformed."

"Hunh. I'm sure he mentioned you studying law at Oxford."

After a lengthy pause, David said, "Look, I don't want to be rude..."

"But you'd really rather I didn't fill the air with pointless chatter."

He frowned. "Did I say that?"

"Yep. I think you passed 'rude' a while back."

He sighed. "It's just that something that might help us to deal together is if we both try to remember that this arrangement of ours is little more than a business accommodation. I can't think you're really all that interested in whether I graduated from Oxford. You're just trying to...be sociable, to show an interest in me. Which under other circumstances would be fine. Commendable even. But for the purposes for our...arrangement, it just isn't necessary, and perhaps it would be best if we simply relieved ourselves of the burden of having to converse nonstop whenever we find ourselves together. How would that be?"

"Okaaay..."

Fine, if that was the way he wanted it. It was good, really. Excellent. Definitely a good thing. What had she been thinking of, anyway, trying to draw him out? She would be expected to reveal things about herself in return, which would mean making stuff up about being a model—an unnerving prospect given that a) she knew less than nothing about the modeling business and b) she'd never had the stomach for out-and-out lying.

Granted, she was lying by omission simply by letting him think she was a model, but her guilt was ameliorated somewhat by David's very unapproachability. He'd told her in so many words that he didn't want to know anything about her. Why, then, should she feel bad about not fessing up?

Not that he'd be that interested even if she did. David Waite was just about the most remote human being she'd ever encountered. She thought about Harlan's advice to stop putting up walls with men, but something told her that no amount of openness on her part could ever get a chilly piece of work like David Waite to want to get to know the real her. He might find her—or rather, the package she came in—sexually appealing in his own indifferent way, but that was as far as it would ever go with him.

And that would never, of course, be far enough for her.

Waite cleared his throat, seeming decidedly ill at ease for a man who'd just delivered a mandate on the subject of needless conversation. "So, do we have an understanding?"

"That I'm to keep my mouth shut when we're alone?"

she said. "Your wish is my command. I'm just the geisha du jour."

He cast her a swift, curious glance, as if she'd said something odd, then lapsed into a contemplative silence and remained that way until they got to the museum.

YOUR WISH IS MY COMMAND. I'm just the geisha du jour.

All through the jazz concert and the cocktail reception that followed, David couldn't stop thinking about what she'd said.

Nor could he stop staring at her—covertly, he hoped—as she accompanied him on his networking circuit among the hundreds of well-heeled art lovers who'd gathered in the museum's elegant Sette MoMA restaurant to help support the building of new additions to this cultural institution.

Right now he stood outside in the moonlit sculpture garden adjacent to the restaurant, where he'd retreated to nurse a Scotch in blessed solitude as he evaluated this intriguing new wrinkle. From his corner of the garden, he could look through the wall of windows into the warmly lit restaurant and watch Nora smile that incandescent smile of hers as Carrie and Mina, Beryl Van Aucken's gauntly chic, ginger-haired daughters, cooed over her jewelry. He couldn't imagine a better model to display it—to display anything. Nora Armstrong could wear a feed sack down the runway, and the buyers would be lining up to place orders.

Tonight, in addition to the rather extraordinary jewelry, which resembled bits of crushed ice imbedded in a network of silver vines, she wore a poured-on skim of dove-gray lace sprinkled with glittery little beads that flickered just slightly with every move she made. The dress was short, revealing mile-high legs rendered all the more shapely by a pair of silver spike heels. Her luminous good looks, her height and those bountiful curves conspired with her provocative attire to make her, yet again, the most resplendent creature in the room.

A resplendent creature who had, unless he was sorely mistaken, offered herself to him in the car on the way here.

I'm just the geisha du jour.

Wandering over to a bench, David sat and lit a cigarette. In the plume of smoke that drifted into the cool night air, a face materialized, a face of porcelain beauty and shyly laughing eyes, the face of the geisha Mutsumi.

During the year David had lived in Tokyo after dropping out of Oxford, the geisha tradition had been one of the aspects of Japanese culture that had most fascinated him. Being young and in poor command of his passions, he'd spent rather more time than he ought to have in one particular teahouse—because that was where he would find Mutsumi. For weeks he'd wooed her in vain, only to discover that she was being kept by a powerful electronics magnate and was therefore available only for such platonic entertainments as pouring his tea and smiling at his clumsy Japanese. Nearly all the girls, he discovered, had wealthy protectors who kept them in luxury in return for their sexual fidelity. Traditional geishas were not prostitutes—if one defined a prostitute as a woman who sold herself on the street, or in some knocking-shop—but they were, for the most part, courtesans.

And now Nora Armstrong was offering to be his "geisha du jour." Did she realize what that implied?

From where he sat, he could still see her, taking cards from both sisters, presumably to pass on to her jewelry-making friend. The little group was soon joined by Beryl Van Aucken and her son, accompanied tonight by Patsy

Crane in her ubiquitous little black dress and string of pearls, her auburn hair adorned by a simple velvet head-band. Alec held Patsy's hand in his, David was amused to note, and it was clear that he only had eyes for her, Nora's resplendence notwithstanding. David wondered how long it would take him to come to his senses and re-alize he couldn't live without her.

Returning his attention to Nora, David took another sip of his Scotch, another slow drag of his cigarette.

What was it she'd said last week at the Red Cross ben-efit? *My function tonight is to be every man's fantasy date, decorative and acquiescent.*

Exactly how much of every man's fantasy was she pre-pared to fulfill, he wondered, letting his gaze linger over the rise of her breasts, the curve of her hip. Just how ac-quiescent was she willing to be?

At lunch yesterday, he had questioned Harlan about his cousin's willingness to keep up her end of the arm candy bargain. Did she understand what was expected of her? David had asked, meaning would she keep a low profile, that sort of thing.

I've talked to her, Harlan had said. *She knows the score. She'll aim to please. You won't be disappointed.*

David had wondered about the sensuality that infused Nora's every gesture, every look. Harlan must have asked her to crank up the seduction throttle to maxi-mum—to reel him in and land him. Of course. The more...accommodating she made herself, the more in-debted David would be, and the more likely to add Har-lan to his regular stable of event planners.

Nora's willingness to essentially prostitute herself for her cousin—in return, apparently, for some past gener-osity of his—was but one more thread in a web of debts and obligations that grew progressively more Byzantine.

I owe him big-time, she'd said. *I'd do anything for Harlan, anything at all.*

Evidently. The only question now was what he, David, intended to do about that.

A column of ash fell onto his trousers. He brushed it off and lit a new cigarette off the old one.

David had paid for sex a handful of times, in foreign cities, for the novelty, but in general he avoided the practice; in truth, he had little need of it, sex never having been very hard to come by in his charmed life. What Nora was offering amounted to sex for remuneration, but instead of paying her, David would be expected to utilize Harlan's services, which, in fact, he'd started doing already, albeit on a trial basis. If Nora was willing to use her body to influence him into making it more permanent, was there any point to be served in refusing her?

Considering the problems he'd had with women of late, such a quid pro quo arrangement actually held a certain measure of appeal. He could obtain relief from the sexual frustration that held him in its grip after five months of abstinence, but without the wrenching melodrama of emotional involvement. Nora wouldn't be pretending to care for him, as had Helena and the others. There would be no lies, no empty promises, no grotesque *scenes*. It would be a purely physical relationship, devoid of strong feelings or the pretense thereof.

It would be perfect.

He'd have to come up with some excuse to ask her up to his apartment the first time, just for the sake of appearances, although it wouldn't have to be anything particularly ingenious; who'd be kidding whom? She had probably been wondering why he hadn't brought her home after the Red Cross benefit. Perhaps she'd giggled to Harlan afterward about how slow on the uptake David had been, prompting Harlan to drop those heavy hints at lunch, which Nora had reinforced in the car with that "geisha du jour" comment.

David took a last drag on his cigarette, his gaze riveted on Nora as she laughed at something Beryl had said. She had a breathy laugh that sometimes had an undercurrent almost like a little growl of pleasure; it made him wonder what she sounded like when she had a man inside her. Did she cry out when she came?

Tonight, he resolved, swallowing down the remainder of his Scotch, *I shall find out.*

6

NORA DIDN'T SAY one single word to David during the drive that night to his apartment on Central Park West. Ever since he'd laid down the law about conversation, she had made a point of volunteering absolutely none of it.

It was a dense, unwieldy silence—they didn't know each other well enough for it to be even remotely "companionable"—and she sensed it was starting to get to him. He seemed edgy and preoccupied, and couldn't stop stealing furtive little glances at her as he drove.

Even when he'd spoken to her directly, she'd offered only monosyllabic answers in return—not glumly, but in a serenely neutral way, as if it made no difference to her whether they talked. That was why, when he'd asked her if she'd mind stopping by his place so he could give her a list of invitees for the *Little Exes* thing to pass on to Harlan, she'd said simply, "Okay," instead of asking why he had to give it to her now, when Harlan wouldn't even be back in town for another two weeks.

He parked the Jag and led her into an imposing stone edifice with The Rialto carved above the front door, the lobby of which—with its mahogany paneling, worn leather furniture and crackled old oil paintings of Venice—looked a lot like one of those fusty English men's clubs redolent of cigar smoke and port.

"Good evening, Tom," David said to the burly uniformed doorman as he led Nora toward the elevator.

Tom smiled and nodded. "Evenin', Mr. Waite. Miss."

The Rialto's capacious elevator, also mahogany paneled, took them to the fifth floor, where she followed David down a carpeted hallway to apartment 5E. Nora had a pretty clear picture in her mind of what she would find inside, but when David ushered her in and flipped on a pair of wall sconces, she ended up wrong on all counts.

She'd expected his place to be palatial in size and tastefully decorated in antiques, as befitted that aristocratic Victorian throwback thing he had going on. What she found was a really rather small apartment—three or four rooms, max—which, although it featured high ceilings, elaborate moldings and a marble mantel over the fireplace, was in fact sparsely furnished, mostly with classic modern pieces.

In lieu of a living room rug, he'd laid some sort of primitive-looking mat over the parquet floor. And everywhere—on every wall and tabletop—were displayed remarkable examples of indigenous arts and crafts. There were African masks, Chinese scrolls, Navajo pottery, even a cluster of something that looked, for the life of her, like voodoo dolls.

"May I take your jacket?"

She flinched and spun around, not having realized he was right behind her. He'd already shed his topcoat and dinner jacket, leaving him in shirtsleeves and narrow suspenders, the most casual she'd ever seen him. "Um..." Why did he want to take her jacket? She hadn't expected this to be more than a quick stop on her way home.

"I'll pour you something to drink while I look for that list," he said, sliding her jacket off and laying it and her purse on a sleek black leather Barcelona chair that stood against a wall. "Scotch, sherry, vodka…?"

Her scalp tickled; why was he being so civil? "Nothing for me, thanks." This didn't seem like a good time to be blunting her senses with alcohol.

Amusement lit his eyes. "That was nearly a complete sentence. Is it too much to hope that this marks the end of the silent treatment?"

"I understood you'd put a moratorium on conversation."

"Ah, yes, my wish is your command." He smiled then, a too-knowing smile that implied some sort of secret knowledge between them—almost a smile of anticipation. "Now that I know how literally you interpret that, I'll be more careful what I wish for."

As Nora was trying to digest that, he said, "Are you sure I can't bring you something? A glass of wine…?"

"Pop, if you've got it."

"If you mean minerals—cola, that sort of thing—I'm afraid I don't have any. I've got some soda water. Will that do?"

"Yes. Thank you."

While David was in the kitchen pouring her drink, from one of those old-fashioned soda siphons, it sounded like, Nora snooped around a bit.

He had no television, unless there was one in the bedroom, but there was a state-of-the-art sound system and, sitting incongruously on a rolltop desk in the corner, a fax machine. The only hint of clutter, if you could call it that, were the monumental stacks of books—overflow, evidently, from the many built-in bookshelves. Perusing one stack, she found a history of the East India Company, a comparative religion text, a biography of John D. Rockefeller and a good deal of fiction, some of it in languages other than English. She scooped up a handful of the foreign novels.

"Find anything interesting?" David asked as he emerged from the kitchen with her glass of seltzer in one hand and what looked like whiskey on the rocks in the other. He looked even more at home than before, having rolled up his sleeves, removed his bow tie and unbuttoned his shirt collar.

"Do you actually read Italian?" she asked, holding up an Umberto Eco title.

"Yes."

She flipped to another. "What's this, Japanese?"

"Yes. And yes, I can read it, but just barely."

She squinted at the lettering on the third book, a slightly musty-smelling old leather-bound volume.

"Ancient Greek. Yes." He held out her drink, which she set the books down to take. "Cheers."

Nora closed her eyes as she sipped, relishing the fragrance of the chunk of lime he'd added to the seltzer, a nice touch. He wasn't just being civil, he was being downright pleasant. Something was seriously out of whack here.

When she opened her eyes, she found him contemplating her over the rim of his glass with that dark, penetrating gaze of his. A little shiver coursed through her, whether from the icy drink or him, she couldn't say.

She yelped as something brushed against her leg.

"You're skittish tonight." Setting his drink down, he scooped up the biggest, fluffiest cat she'd ever seen, a gigantic slate-gray puffball with sleepy yellow eyes. "Hortense, shame on you. You've startled our guest." An ecstatic, grinding purr rose from the animal as David cradled her in his arms, burying his fingers in her fur as

he petted her. She yawned, displaying a mouthful of nee-
dle-sharp teeth.

Nora backed up a step and sipped her drink, her gaze
fixed on the cat in case it decided to leap at her.

"You're not afraid of cats, are you?" he asked.

"No, not...exactly." But she'd never liked them, even
the barn cats back home, which at least made themselves
useful by catching mice, although she hated to watch
them at work. "It's just that they're so...sly and—I don't
know—vicious."

"They're predators," he said, scratching Hortense behind the ears. "It's in their nature to be sly and vicious."

"They're needlessly cruel. Have you ever watched one
toying with some helpless little animal before going in
for the kill?"

"Yes. I find it fascinating."

You would.

"Here." Reaching out, he captured her free hand and
brought it toward the cat.

"No, no, no, no, no." Nora tensed, tried to pull back,
but David's grip was far too strong for that.

"Relax," he said in that toe-curling voice as he forced
her hand open and flattened it onto the cat's enormous
white stomach. Entwining his fingers with hers, he
guided her hand in a rhythmic pattern that Hortense apparently loved, given the escalating resonance of her
purring.

Nora did relax. The warmth of David's hand, and of
the animals's belly, seemed to flow up her arm and into
her chest. She savored the contrast of Hortense's impossibly downy fur with David's slightly callused flesh.
Their hands weren't moving anymore, she realized. His
fingers stroked hers just slightly, a subtle caress.

When she looked up, he was staring at her again, his gaze lighting on her hair, her eyes, her mouth.

Oh.

He moved fractionally closer.

Oh.

Sliding her hand out from beneath his, she turned and took a few steps away, mechanically sipping from her glass while she sorted through what was happening here.

He was coming on to her.

He couldn't be coming on to her. They had an understanding.

He'd meant to kiss her. If she hadn't moved away, he would have kissed her.

Might have.

Would have.

She heard a soft thud behind her. David must have set the cat down.

A weighty moment of silence passed, and then he said, "Here, let me give you this."

Nora looked back over her shoulder as he went to the roll-top desk, unlatched a briefcase lying next to the fax machine and began rummaging through it. Good. He'd give her the list now, and then he'd drive her home, and that would be that.

She crossed to the Barcelona chair, set her glass on an end table and lifted her jacket and purse. When she looked up, she was face-to-face with her own reflection on a collection of about two dozen small pictures framed under glass and arranged close together on the wall above the chair. It was an eclectic mix, with most of the pieces obviously very old and valuable—Japanese woodblocks, American folk art, a little half-finished pastel of a woman bathing that could have been a Degas and maybe was, a page from a medieval illuminated manuscript, a Byzantine icon, a sepia-tinted photograph of African tribesmen that must have dated from the last century....

Directly in front of her was a very small painting that looked Indian in origin. A man in a red turban and a woman with black hair and sultry, kohl-edged eyes were embracing on a heap of multicolored pillows, their gazes locked in passion, their braceleted limbs entangled, their garments in disarray....

Nora blinked at the little painting, focusing on a gap in their robes. It wasn't just their gazes that were locked, she saw. They were coupling in a way she had never imagined before, the man caressing the woman's bare breasts, her arms curving over her head in evident bliss.

The unusual position intrigued Nora. Heck, the *missionary* position intrigued her. Not that she'd ever get to experience either one, at the rate she was going.

Part of her had wanted David to kiss her—and more. She ached to feel the heat of his mouth, the restless caress of his hands. Many times during this past week she'd imagined what it would be like to make love to him, to be an object of desire and affection to a man like David Waite. How would it feel to be the recipient of his passions—passions that she suspected ran deep, despite his facade of urbane unflappability?

Yet she had turned away just when it looked as if she might find out.

It's a vicious circle, Harlan had said. If a man showed a little interest in her, she concluded it was simple lust and backed away, which meant he never got to know the real her, which made relationships impossible, which meant that she was doomed to perpetual virginity.

Why had she burned David off just now? Force of habit, to some extent, and the fact that he made her nervous as hell, but for the most part, it was plain old shock. After all his bellyaching about the arm candy ground rules, she hadn't expected him to just blithely disregard the most fundamental one—that their relationship was to remain platonic.

But if he was violating their understanding, he must have decided to amend the rules. Her knee-jerk reaction was to blame it on the lust factor, but maybe Harlan was right; maybe she should give a guy the benefit of the doubt.

Especially this guy.

Was it possible he was coming to feel the same complicated mix of fascination and yearning toward her that she felt toward him? This electricity between them, this strange and wonderful enchantment, couldn't be one-sided. Could it?

Well, maybe it could, but it probably wasn't, and shouldn't she give him the chance to show that he felt something, too—something for her as a person, not just her body? She'd never been so intrigued by a man, so utterly spellbound. And she did not, after all, want to die a virgin.

"Here it is," he said. In the glass over the pictures, she watched him walk toward her from across the room. He had something in his hand; she couldn't quite make it out, but it wasn't a piece of paper. "Do you like art?" Coming up behind her, he ran his fingertips lightly down her left arm, making her heart skitter wildly.

Ah. He hasn't given up.

So rattled was she by his touch, and the knowledge of where it would inevitably lead if she let it, that she almost blurted out the truth—that her college experience had, in addition to teaching her how to manipulate metals, instilled in her an appreciation for art that had lain dormant during a childhood spent feeding and milking cows. But that was her real background. Nora Armstrong, High-Fashion Model, would have spent the past five years perfecting her camera pout and runway strut, not learning about things like aluminum anodization and electroforming and stone setting.

"I do like art," she said. "This is an amazing collection."

"Thank you." He stroked her right arm now, his touch so whisper light that all her nerve endings seemed to quiver on end. Looking down, she saw that it wasn't his fingertips caressing her so airily, but feathers—the feathers on the end of the hair pick she'd lost in his car.

"You found it," she said.

"Mmm...I was almost tempted not to give it back." He trailed the tuft of feathers up her arm and over her shoulder. Bypassing the necklace, he drew it softly over the swells of her upper breasts.

She clutched her jacket and purse as if they were lifelines. "Is that a Degas?" she asked, nodded toward the exquisite, half-drawn nude.

"Yes."

"It's beautiful."

"You would have been a good model for him," David said, his voice low, resonant, a seductive vibration that made her feel light-headed. She felt the cool silk of his shirt against the bare upper half of her back, the fine wool of his trousers against her stockinged legs. He was standing close, she realized, very close. With the chair right in front of her and David behind, she had the sense of being trapped, but the panic that speeded her heart only intensified her heady anticipation.

"No, not Degas," he murmured into her hair as he trailed the feathered pick downward over her breast. Although she could barely feel it, it made her nipples prickle beneath the confines of her satin bra. "Ingres," he said. "Ingres should have painted you. He could have captured your voluptuousness. And that glow to your skin, that inner radiance. And your eyes, the way you look right at a man—into him."

David met her eyes in their reflection; she held his gaze for a long, breathless moment. Taking her purse out of her hand, he slipped the hair pick into it and tossed it on the chair, followed by her jacket.

He bent his head. She felt the hot tickle of his lips on the back of her neck, and again, and again...and then he closed his hands over her breasts.

She watched, transfixed, as he squeezed her lightly through her clothes, weighing her fullness, rubbing his thumbs over her rigid nipples as he pulled her back against the hard wall of his chest. "You are so incredibly beautiful. I've wanted to touch you this way since the first time I saw you."

He sounded almost winded. She felt his breathing increase in tempo, felt a sense of urgency in his caress. Lifting one hand, he tugged the straps of her dress and bra down over one shoulder, slid his hand beneath the loosened garments and cupped her aching flesh.

She flinched in startled pleasure when he pinched her nipple. "Easy," he murmured as he alternately tormented and soothed her with those long, clever fingers. "Easy."

He gathered up her skirt with his other hand, which roamed upward over the band of lace at the top of her thigh-high stocking until it met her bare upper leg. He gave a little growl deep in his throat when he glided his hand over her bottom, finding it naked except for the slimmest of satin thongs. Nora bit her lip to keep from gasping at the rough warmth of his touch on her softest flesh.

She gazed at their reflection with a sense of strange, almost drugged detachment, as if her body, although it hummed with desire, belonged not to her, but to some tall blond model wearing a little too much makeup and a come-hither dress. She watched as David, still caressing her breast, smoothed his other hand over her hip and belly until it encountered the front panel of her thong.

He paused, watching the reflection of his own hand as it molded to the strip of white satin, one finger stroking her lightly, teasingly. Her heart thudded painfully in her chest; it was all she could do to fetch her breath.

He pressed himself against her from behind, and that was when she realized he was as deeply aroused as she. She'd never felt a man's erection before. Even through their clothes, it felt as hard as a column of steel. Her gaze strayed to the little Indian painting and the tiny, almost unnoticeable gap in the couple's robes, through which the man could be seen half-sheathed within the woman.

David moved against her as she contemplated the double exposure of their image over that of the couple in the painting. The woman's expression as she gazed into her lover's eyes was rapturous. What did it feel like, Nora wondered, to take a man inside her, to feel him stroking her from within as their mutual pleasure escalated?

She would find out soon enough.

Raising his hand, David slipped his fingers under the satin cord that formed the thong's waistband, then beneath the panel. She hitched in her breath as he touched her where no man had ever touched her before.

"You're still skittish, Miss Armstrong," he murmured. "Go with it. Relax into it."

Nora's sensual delirium evaporated almost instantly. She gripped his hand, stilling him.

"Miss Armstrong?" she said.

He met her eyes in the reflection. "That *is* your name."

"My name is Nora."

He seemed to think about that for a moment. "Fine, then. I'll call you Nora, all right?"

"No." She pulled his hand out of her thong, wrested the other from her breast. Sidestepping out of his embrace, her back to him, she hastily righted her disheveled clothing. "No," she said shakily, "it's not all right. You're just humoring me." She turned to face him. "How could you call me 'Miss Armstrong' while you were...were..."

He raised a hand. "All right, now, calm—"

"What was it you said in the car tonight? 'Best to keep things on an impersonal footing?' That's why you call me Miss Armstrong, isn't it? To keep this—" she gestured between the two of them "—us...impersonal?"

He dragged a hand through his hair. "That's right."

"You had your hands all over me!" she shouted, shaking with rage. "Don't you think that's pretty freakin' personal?"

"Not necessarily, no."

"*What?*"

He let out an exasperated sigh. "I did hope, given the nature of...our arrangement, that we could maintain a certain perspective about the...physical aspect, not muddy it up with all sorts of..." He frowned as if groping for words.

It really was just the package he was lusting after, and not *her*. He'd only been acting nice so that she'd let down her guard before he went in for the kill. Or maybe he'd just been toying with his prey, like the cats he so admired.

For the first time in her life, she'd given a man the benefit of the doubt and let him close, only to discover he didn't feel anything for her, nothing at all. God forbid she should try and hold a conversation with him, but she was expected to lie down and spread her legs for him? She stared at him, so coldly handsome, so aloof, and wondered if he'd ever had feelings for anybody.

"You're not even human." She gathered up her jacket and purse and headed for the door. "I'll get a cab downstairs."

He leapt across the living room after her, slamming his hands on the door to either side of her head just as she reached for the knob. Steeling herself, she turned to face him, holding her jacket and purse in front of her like a shield. Unruly tendrils of hair fell over his brow; his eyes glinted darkly.

"I'm all too human, Miss Armstrong," he said in a soft, strained voice, "and I can only be pushed so far."

7

"LET ME GO," she said unsteadily.

David strove for composure, when all he really wanted was to shove her dress up and take her, right here against this door. In as civil a tone as he could muster, he said, "Don't come the innocent with me. We both know why you let me bring you up here."

"Where do you get your gall?" she demanded, the very picture of outrage.

"Look, if it's my calling you Miss Armstrong that's got your knickers in a twist, I'll call you whatever you bloody..." He closed his eyes for a moment, clenched his jaw. "Whatever you want, all right? Just don't ask me to feign an intimacy that doesn't exist. That would insult us both."

Why she'd gone off at half cock this way, in the midst of all that exquisite heat and passion, was a mystery to David. All right, he supposed he'd dropped a brick, calling her Miss Armstrong while he had his hand down her knickers, but considering this was more or less a barter arrangement, why should she really care what he called her? Unless...

Unless it was just an act, an effort to spice things up a bit...not that they'd needed spicing up, God knew, but it had been his experience that some women liked to stir the pot a little. Or perhaps, in livening up their prearranged tryst this way, she was trying to give him his money's worth, so to speak. If that was the case, he could play along—anything, just to get things back on course again. He'd never been so wild to have a woman; he wasn't about to let her get so caught up in her performance that she actually stormed away.

"You're not going anywhere." He tugged her jacket and purse out of her hand and set them on the little table next to the door. "You know the score—don't pretend you don't."

"I don't know what you're talking about." Pushing on his chest, she tried to squirm away from him. He seized her around the waist and pressed her against the door.

"You made your deal with the devil," he said, letting a hint of menace creep into his voice, which should help to satisfy her desire for drama. "I seem to recall your promising to keep to it." Holding her still with one hand, he pulled her skirt up with the other.

"This wasn't the deal I made." She grabbed his hands and tried in vain to wrest them away.

"Wasn't it?" He hooked a finger in the waistband of her thong and started sliding it down.

"Damn it, no!" In an unexpected display of fury, Nora lashed out with her fists, pummeling his face. One blow caught him on the nose, igniting a bolt of pain that sent him stumbling backward. "It wasn't!"

David's nose pulsed with pain; his cheek stung. He stared at her incomprehensibly as she snatched up her purse with quavering hands and pulled out the hair pick. "Keep away from me," she ordered shakily, brandishing the pick like a weapon.

No. Oh, no. No. This had to be part of her little game. He couldn't have misread the situation this badly.

"All right." David took a step toward her, hands raised placatingly. "Look. Just—"

"Just *stay back!*" Reaching behind her, she opened the door and backed out into the passage. "I'll put this in your eye, I swear I will!" She was shaking from head to toe; tears trembled in her eyes.

No, he thought as a sick tide of comprehension swept over him. "Please," he said very softly, "just listen to—"

"Don't you ever come near me again." She slammed the door.

Silence roared. David stared in numb horror at the closed door, his hands still upraised. From out in the hallway, he heard the door to the lift open and close.

Please don't let me have done this.

"Oh, no," he moaned, clawing both hands through his hair. "You idiot. You blighter. You stupid, stupid, stupid, stupid ass."

You did it, all right. You lured an unsuspecting woman up here on false pretenses and mauled her. And when she tried to flee, you threatened to force yourself on her.

What was the matter with him? What had he become, that he could have done this? He'd obviously misinterpreted the situation to a grotesque degree. Had he wanted her so desperately that he'd become blind to all reason?

Yes.

Was that an excuse?

Unequivocally, no.

"Bloody hell." He had to find her, explain things to her, make it right.

Yanking the door open, he raced into the hall and down the fire stairs to the lobby, where he found Tom leaning against the wall reading one of his paperbacks.

"Did you see her?" David rasped. "My...er...Miss—"

"Mr. Waite!" The brawny night doorman frowned at

him open-mouthed. "What happened to your face? D'you know you're bleedin'?"

"Did you see her?" David screamed.

"The lady you come in with earlier?"

"Yes. Yes."

"Sure, she come tearin' through here like a bat outa hell about a minute ago. I called to her, but she didn't even slow down."

"Did you notice where she went?" David asked, crossing to the front door.

"'Fraid not. I'm...kinda caught up here," Tom said sheepishly, holding up the book, one of those series romances. They're just about to...you know."

Hope the bloke in that book is a bit swifter than I was, David thought as he stepped through the front door onto the sidewalk, illuminated by street lamps and nearly deserted. Traffic was, likewise, sparse on Central Park West at this time of night. There was no sign of Nora in either direction, though as he was turning his head, he fancied he saw a flicker of movement across the street in the Women's Gate—the Seventy-second Street entrance to Central Park.

Walking over to the curb, he looked across the avenue at the great park, proximity to which contributed to the astronomical prices of co-op apartments in the venerable old Rialto. As pleasant as the park could be during the day, no one of sound mind, particularly a lone woman, would take a casual stroll through it at night, when the street rats were on the prowl. Everyone who'd lived in this city for any length of time at all knew about Central Park at night.

David tried to recall what Harlan had told him about Nora. She'd been living in Milan of late. He remembered that, because he'd lived in Milan himself once; if this were a normal relationship, he would have mentioned that to Nora by now, and they would have compared notes. But before Milan, she'd been a New Yorker...hadn't she? David couldn't recall Harlan's having explicitly said that, although it was the impression he'd come away with.

She wouldn't have gone into the park. She had no reason to do so, and besides, she would have known better. That glimmer of movement could have been no more than his wishful imagination. Or it could have been a junkie looking for someone to roll.

A taxi swerved toward him and slowed down, its driver having apparently noticed him standing on the curb. David waved him on and sprinted across the street and through the Women's Gate.

He paused a few yards in, where the road met a bridle path, pondering which direction she might have gone if she had come in here. *She didn't come in here. This is pointless. You're just inviting a mugging.* Having conducted a hands-on study of street fighting in some of the world's most treacherous back alleys, David wasn't concerned for himself; his size alone tended to act as a deterrent. But Nora, in her slinky little dress and high heels, would be a tempting target indeed.

He jogged north for a ways along the dirt track, scanning Strawberry Fields to the left and the woods to the right, looking for any sign of movement in the dark. Nothing. Heading south, he searched the loop road and the network of intersecting paths in this section of the park, but came up empty.

She wasn't in the park, he concluded when he found himself back at the Women's Gate. She wouldn't have come in here. He was wasting his time. Most likely she'd lucked into a cab as soon as she stepped out of his building. She had her purse with her; she'd have money and keys. She'd be fine. Or as fine as she could be, after he'd all but raped her.

You really blew it this time, Waite.

David patted his trouser pocket, hoping he'd remembered to transfer his cigarettes and lighter into it when he took his jacket off. He had. He lit a cigarette and smoked it while he walked back across the street, snuffing it out in the Italianate urn of sand that served as an ashtray outside the Rialto.

Tom held the door open for him. "Everything all right, Mr. Waite?"

"I, uh...I think so." Turning, David scrutinized the area one last time. No shimmer of blond hair, no flash of silvery lace. The night had turned chilly; he felt it now that he was standing still. She'd left her jacket upstairs in his apartment.

She'll be fine, he assured himself as he went inside and headed for the lift. By now she was already at her cousin's apartment. David would ring her up tomorrow, explain things, sort it all out; better yet, go down to Chelsea and do it in person. Perhaps, when he'd made her understand what a monstrous misunderstanding it had all been, what a ludicrous comedy of errors, they might even laugh about it.

Don't count on it, you sorry git.

NORA STOOD SHIVERING in the dark at the convergence of two of the park's smaller, unlit paths—or was it three?—wondering where in hell she was and why she couldn't manage to find her way back to where she'd come in, and reflecting that she really had made a terrible, terrible, terrible mistake, coming to New York.

A gust of wind made the leaves on the surrounding

trees rattle ominously. A leaf struck her face; she flinched and dropped her purse and the hair pick.

She scooped up the purse, but the pick had rolled away on the trail of packed earth. As she dropped to her knees to search for it, she heard a faint chuckling sound from somewhere nearby. Some sort of bird, probably. Or some other small animal. Definitely not human.

Probably not human.

Oh, God, what was she doing here?

Avoiding David Waite, that's what. On leaving his building, she'd crossed to the other side of the street, where there seemed to be a greater concentration of taxis passing by. When David had emerged from the Rialto's front door not a minute later, looking around for her, she'd ducked into the park.

Great, she'd thought. *First it's attempted date rape. Now he's stalking me.*

Seized with alarm when he crossed the street and headed right for her, she'd turned and run down the nearest path. She'd heard rapid footsteps behind her— his, no doubt—and detoured into the woods, where she'd wandered for awhile in a state of mounting panic, only to finally stumble across another little path, which led to another, and another. Every fork in the road had been a new opportunity to get more hopelessly lost, which was what she was now.

Lost and cold and terrified. She would almost prefer David Waite's Bachelor Pad of Horrors to this. *Out of the frying pan, into the fire.*

Groping in the dirt on her hands and knees, she heard it again, the chuckle. It *was* a chuckle, a man's chuckle, deep and slightly lascivious. And very, very close.

"Lose somethin', baby?"

Out of the darkness in front of her there coalesced a

darker shape, huge and hulking, a man sauntering toward her. A spot of orange glowed near his hand—a joint, from the smell of the smoke.

This isn't happening. This can't be happening.

"Maybe me and my friend can help you." The orange spot dropped to the ground and winked out.

From behind came the sound of a belt being unbuckled.

Nora tried to scramble to her feet, but the man from behind was on her in a heartbeat, crushing her facedown into the dirt. He reeked of marijuana, beer and sour sweat.

"Not so fast," he rasped into her ear as he unzipped his fly. "You haven't found what you came lookin' for yet."

8

THE PHONE ON David's bedside locker rang.

He blinked and looked down at the Scotch bottle tucked into his fist as he sat leaning against the bedhead, still half-dressed, every light in the bedroom blazing.

Let it ring. He had no desire to talk to anybody. Unless...

It might be Nora. He reached for the phone, but stilled his hand. She wouldn't be calling him, not after what he'd done to her tonight. Considering the hour—his bedside clock said it was 1:37 a.m.—chances were it was a crank call.

It rang again. He'd let the machine get it. If by some fluke, it was Nora, he'd pick up.

He felt dazed, but not drunk. Had he consumed any of the Scotch? He didn't think so. The cap was still screwed on. Couldn't even manage to do that right.

He'd come back upstairs after his unsuccessful search for Nora determined to drink himself into a reeling stupor. It was the only way he'd be able to put aside his self-flagellation long enough to get any sleep tonight. Instead, he seemed to have spent the past hour staring into space and wishing he was dead.

Lowering his bare feet to the carpet, he caught sight of his reflection in the full-length glass on the back of his bedroom door. He looked the very personification of scruffy decadence, with his shirt hanging open, braces dangling and hair wildly unkempt—and gripping a bottle of booze, no less. A raw scratch traversed his cheek, a souvenir of Nora's ring, no doubt, when she'd clocked him; thankfully, his nose, although it still ached, appeared to be unbroken.

He didn't look much like the Lord High Control Freak tonight.

The phone rang a third time, and then the answering machine kicked in: "David Waite here. Leave a message at the tone."

The machine beeped, and there came the sound of a man mumbling something. Good Lord, it *was* a crank call, David thought, until he became aware that the man was saying, under his breath, "Mr. Waite...pick up! *Please* pick up."

He lifted the receiver. "Hello?"

"Thank God," the voice whispered. "Mr. Waite, it's me—Tom."

Tom? Ah—the night doorman downstairs. But... "Tom, why are you phoning me? Why not use the intercom?"

"'Cause she thinks I'm callin' a—"

"Speak up. I can barely—"

"I can't let her hear me. She thinks I'm callin' her a cab. If she catches on that I'm talkin' to you, I think she'll bolt. She told me not to let you know she was here. All's she wants is a cab."

"She?" David sprang to his feet. "You mean—"

"The blonde, the one you were askin' about before."

"She's there? In the lobby? Now?"

"Yeah, but I gotta tell you—"

"I'll be right down."

"Wait!" Tom rasped. "Wait a minute, Mr. Waite. I think you should know she's...she's not in too good a shape." He paused. "She was...attacked. In the park, she said. I'm sorry, man. I think she was..." He let out a breath.

No. God, no.

"Her clothes are ripped," Tom continued, "and she's all bleedin'—"

David dropped the phone and the bottle, tore through his apartment, out the door, down the fire stairs, shirttails flying, heart pounding.

He hurtled into the lobby, looking around wildly. Tom, pacing anxiously by the front door, caught his eye and looked meaningfully toward a leather club chair, where the top of a blond head was just visible.

David drew in a deep breath and let it out. On silent feet he circled the chair and stood before her.

Nora sat curled up with her eyes closed, battered and filthy, her hair loose and tangled with leaves, bloody scrapes showing through the ladders in her stockings. She had one arm wrapped tightly around her; with the other hand she was clutching both the bodice of her shredded dress and her purse, which he was astounded she'd managed to hang on to.

David felt as if he'd been kicked in the stomach. "Oh, Nora."

Her eyes snapped open. He took a step toward her. She shrank back and looked toward Tom, clearly shaken. "You called him? You said—"

"I'm sorry, Miss," Tom said. "I just thought it would be best if..." He looked helplessly toward David.

"Nora." David reached out to her. "Let me—"

"No!" She swatted his hand away, leapt up out of the chair, made a dash for the front door.

David tackled her before she'd gone two yards, banding his arms around her and easing her onto a couch. She bucked and writhed, tried to punch him again, but he gathered her up tightly, saying, "I can't let you leave, Nora, not in this condition. Please, you've got to let me help you."

"I don't want your help!" she said in a shrill, wavering voice as she continued to thrash, straining against him. "I hate you!"

"That makes two of us. Please, Nora," he said as evenly as he could, "don't struggle like this. Nora. Nora, listen to me. I'm sorry about...before. I was an idiot. I made a mistake, a stupid mistake. I came to the completely wrong conclusion, and now this has happened to you, and it's my fault entirely. I'm sorry, Nora. I'm sorry. I'm sorry..."

He was rocking her, murmuring her name into her hair, which seemed to soothe her; she wasn't fighting him anymore. "I'm so sorry. I'm such an ass. You have every right to be furious with me, and—and afraid of me. Be as angry as you want, but please don't be afraid of me—please. I won't hurt you. I swear to God, I just want to help you. Let me help you."

She had quietened, but was shivering like a bird.

"You won't run if I let you go, will you?" he asked.

After a moment, she shook her head.

He eased back a bit. She looked up at him, wary, but without the dread that had been there when she'd first seen him. Her face was grimy, but he could see only two small abrasions, one above her eye, the other high on her cheek. There were some scratches on her arms, and those scrapes on her legs, but apparently no broken bones or major lacerations.

Not that she hadn't been brutalized. Her dress was ripped down the middle; she held the two halves together with a trembling hand, trying futilely to conceal her white satin bra.

He whipped off his shirt and draped it over her. "Here, put this on."

She shook her head. "It'll get blood on it."

"I've got others." He took her purse out of her left hand, set it aside and threaded her arm through a sleeve. When he reached for her right hand, he found it gripped tightly around something—that hair pick. Prying her fingers open, he saw that the pick was a bit worse for wear, its feathers crushed and the pointed end darkly stained. He put it on top of the purse and eased that arm through the sleeve. She pulled the shirt around her and mumbled her thanks.

David gathered her in his arms; she slumped against him, still shivering. He chafed her arms and back.

"They're still out there," she mumbled into his chest.

"They?"

"The two men."

Two? "Oh, Nora, I'm sorry. I'm sorry." He held her tight, kissed her hair. Meeting the doorman's grim gaze over the top of her head, he said, "Tom, call the police. Tell them what happened and ask them to meet us at Columbia-Presbyterian Hospital. I'm going to take her there now."

"What?" She tensed, pulled away from him. "No."

"Nora, you have to report this. They might be able to find the men who did this to you and arrest them. And you need medical attention."

"They're only scratches," she protested. "I hate hospitals."

"I'm not talking about the scratches," he said gently. "After...what happened, you really need to be examined,

Nora—for the sake of your health, and because it might help them to identify who did this to you."

She looked genuinely perplexed.

He wished he didn't have to spell it out. "They will have left their DNA behind."

Her eyes widened in comprehension.

"Nora, I know you must loathe the prospect of being examined like that, after what you've been through, and being interrogated by the police—"

"No. David..."

"But I'll stay with you the whole time—if you'll let me. I'll make sure you're treated—"

"I wasn't raped, David."

He stared at her, relief warring with incredulity. Her dress... "They didn't..."

"They tried. But I had that." She nodded toward the hair pick; it dawned on him what the dark stain was. "I'd lost it on the ground," she said, "but my hand brushed against it just as...just in time. I grabbed it and...used it."

"Thank God." He held her tightly, nuzzling her hair.

Tom crossed himself and shot a fist. "Yes! Hope you made pincushions outa those animals."

"I think I might have really hurt one of them," she said. "The one who was...on top of me. I found the pick just as he turned me over and..." A shudder coursed through her. "And then the other one tried to grab me as I was getting away, and...I guess he didn't expect me to have any kind of weapon. They didn't know what was happening, either one of them. It was dark, and they were stoned, and it all happened so fast. I kicked off my shoes and grabbed my bag and ran like hell."

"That took an awful lot of nerve," David said, genuinely impressed. "And presence of mind. I give you full marks for courage."

"I didn't feel very courageous. I was terrified, even after I left them back there on that path. It seemed like forever before I made my way out of the park, and I was worried they'd come after me. But then I did get out, and I saw the lights on here, and..." She shrugged.

"Come on," David said, smoothing her snarled hair off her face. "We're going upstairs. You can wash up a bit, put your feet up. I'll call this in to the police, and my doctor lives in this building. He can just—"

"I just want to go home," she said listlessly.

"To Chelsea?"

"To Ohio, to my parents' farm." Her chin quivered.

Ohio? "I heard you telling Beryl tonight how much you love New York."

"Not anymore." She shook her head, her eyes shimmering wetly. "Just one damn week in this city, and look what happens. I want to go home."

He stroked her hair. "That's understandable, but perhaps you'll feel differently in a few days. Come upstairs with me."

"No." She took a deep, shaky breath, as if to stave off her impending tears. "I'd rather go back to Chelsea."

"You'd be going back to an empty apartment, Nora. Harlan and Kevin are on holiday. I don't like to think of you being all alone in that great big place tonight, after everything you've been through."

Her brow furrowed as she contemplated that obviously unappealing prospect.

"Stay here tonight," he said.

She darted a quick, apprehensive glance in his direction.

"I'm a cad," he said, "but I'm not a monster. I've subjected you to quite enough unwanted attention for one night. Even I know when to draw the line."

She almost smiled.

"I'll sleep in the living room," he said. "You'll have the bedroom all to yourself."

"What'll you sleep on?" she asked. "I didn't see a couch."

"I've got a tatami." In response to her look of puzzlement, he added, "A Japanese mat made of straw and rushes."

"Of course." She really did smile then, a watery little smile that broke his heart. "You *would* have a tatami."

DAVID KNOCKED SOFTLY on his bedroom door early the next morning—very softly, so as not to rouse Nora if she hadn't awoken yet. He wouldn't be trespassing on her privacy this way, but there was no way to get to the bathroom except through the bedroom.

Hearing no sound from within, he eased the door open and stepped quietly into the room, softly illuminated by morning sunlight streaming between the slats of his bamboo window shades.

Nora lay curled on her side, fast asleep with the covers pushed down to her waist and one arm draped around Hortense, tucked snugly up next to her stomach. It would appear, David thought with a smile, that Nora had made her peace with cats—or at least with the drowsily serene Hortense, one of the most agreeable animals he'd ever known.

Nora looked almost like a little girl in his too-large blue cotton pajamas. Her hair, having been washed right before bed, had dried into prettily haphazard waves while she slept. Her face, scrubbed free of makeup, was luminous and pink cheeked, its sole imperfection being those two small abrasions.

Thank God her only souvenirs of last night's nightmare were a few bumps and scrapes—her only *visible* souvenirs. He hoped the assault in the park, coming as it did on the heels of his own de facto molestation of her, didn't leave her with emotional scars. Somehow he doubted that would be the case. She struck him as exceptionally plucky and resilient, not the type to fold after a traumatic experience. Still, she *had* talked about leaving New York; he had best deal gently with her, at least for a few days.

He'd done his best last night, after bringing her back up here, to make her feel safe and comfortable. His first order of business had been to sit her down, tuck a rug over her and pour her a sherry. She'd sipped it with a glazed expression while he got through to the police, who informed him there was little they could do to apprehend Nora's attackers, since she hadn't gotten a good look at them. He'd rung up Dr. Glass then, who, being the good-natured fellow he was, got out of bed and came over to examine Nora, only to conclude that there were, indeed, no serious injuries.

Nora had been desperate for a bath, wanting to "soak off the feel of their hands." While the tub was filling, David took up a comb and extracted from her hair all the bits of dried leaves and twigs that had gotten tangled in it—not to mention a goodly pile of hair grips. It had never occurred to him that a French twist might require so many pins to hold it together. He took his time at the task, since it seemed to relax her—and since he found it so immensely gratifying just to be able to touch any part of her, to know that she would allow him to, after all that had transpired earlier.

How astounding that he had the power to comfort her; how miraculous that she would let him. And how utterly dumbfounding to feel this urge to care for her, to console and safeguard her. It had been a novel sensation, no other woman he'd known having roused his protective instinct to quite the same level.

Novel and a bit unnerving, considering the emotional investment such an instinct implied.

Very unnerving, given how disastrous such investments had proven for him in the past.

I'm not falling for her, he thought now, *just showing a bit of human compassion. Nothing wrong with that*. As long as he left it at that and didn't let it snowball into something more.

He could manage that, he assured himself as he padded across the bedroom and closed the bathroom door quietly behind him, stealing one last look at the woman sleeping in his bed. All it took was a bit of backbone, and if he had one long suit, it was surely self-restraint.

David flicked on the bathroom light, his gaze automatically zeroing in on the toothbrush holder built into the tiled wall—one of those ceramic rings with four little holes for toothbrushes and a cup holder in the middle. This morning, one hole held his toothbrush, one held the new brush he'd given Nora to use last night, and a third held that deceptively frivolous-looking little hair pick.

On the phone with the police last night, David had offered to bag up the bloodstained pick and turn it in if it would help to capture and convict Nora's assailants. The offer had been rejected on the grounds that DNA identification was far too costly and involved to bother with for a routine attempted rape. It made David's hackles rise to think of this savage attack as "routine," but he knew better than to argue the point. He'd returned the pick to Nora, who had apparently washed it off, fluffed the feathers back up and left it to dry in his toothbrush holder.

He didn't blame her for wanting to clean it up and keep it. The samurai warrior had his *tachi* sword, Hawkeye his flintlock rifle, King Arthur his Excalibur...and Nora Armstrong her jeweled and feathered hair pick. No weapon had ever earned a greater measure of honor in David's eyes.

He turned on the shower and shrugged out of the threadbare old toweling robe he'd thrown on over his boxers in case Nora had been awake. As he was draping it over the hook on the back of the door, he noticed the outline of a packet of Dunhills in one pocket. He pulled them out, flipped the box open; it was half-full.

I kissed a smoker once. I'll never do it again.

David upended the open packet over the toilet, but just as the cigarettes started sliding out, he righted it again.

It wasn't that giving up smoking wasn't a good idea; he might be a nicotine addict, but he wasn't stupid. He knew he should quit.

He just didn't know if he should quit for her. The better part of wisdom at this juncture would be to dial things back to where they'd been before, when Nora was just arm candy and the whole point of the arrangement was to avoid personal entanglements, not encourage them.

He snapped the box shut and returned it to the pocket of his robe.

It was while he was standing under the steamy spray, watching the soapsuds swirling in the drain, that he closed his eyes and allowed himself to remember last night, before he'd made the monumental blunder of calling Nora "Miss Armstrong" at the wrong moment, before everything had gone to hell....

He remembered watching her in the picture glass as she yielded to his touch, her gaze dreamy and unfocused....

He remembered the warmth of her skin, the perfume of her hair, the hot, smooth weight of her breast in his hand....

Her bottom, so impossibly supple, and the damp, intoxicating heat of her through that thin layer of satin. Those shivery little breaths she took when he touched her there. The exquisite anticipation, the heart-pounding promise, the hunger that only she could sate....

"Oh, hell." David turned the faucet just a bit, letting cold water mix with the hot to cool it...and just a bit more, and a bit more, until he felt as if he were back in that half-frozen Siberian lake with those lunatics who fancied brisk midwinter bathes.

He shut off the water, stepped dripping and shivering out of the tub, snatched his cigarettes out of his robe pocket and emptied them into the toilet.

"So much for me writing Act Three," he muttered as he flushed them away.

NORA, SLEEP RUMPLED and bleary and holding Hortense in her arms, found David reading the Sunday *New York Times* with his back to her at the island that took up most of the center of his sunny little kitchen. The clock on the microwave said it was 11:02 a.m. She hadn't slept that late in her entire life, even when she was serving ribs till 2:00 a.m.

"Good morning," she said in a husky, just awakened voice. Hortense jumped to the floor and made a beeline for her food and water in the corner.

"You're up!" David slid his reading glasses off as he rose from his leather-upholstered stool, one of two on this side of the island. He always stood when she entered a room, an outmoded courtesy like opening her car door that was probably politically incorrect, but which she couldn't help liking. The scratch on his cheek looked as if someone had drawn a line on him with a maroon lip pencil.

"You slept well, I hope." He smiled. She'd never seen him smile before, not a real smile like this one. It lightened him, transformed him, made him look like a completely different man, an illusion reinforced by his attire—jeans, sneakers and a faded New York Knicks sweatshirt. Nora found the whole package—the uncombed hair, the morning beard stubble, the smile and the Average Joe getup—something of a shock to the system.

"You must be David Waite's good twin." She held out her hand. "I'm Nora Armstrong."

He actually laughed then, as he took her hand between both of his, a soft, deep chuckle that *really* threw her for a loop. The sound of it touched her like a man's hand—David's hand, warm and slightly scratchy—running all up and down her spine. It had felt the same way last night, when he'd held her and called her Nora over and over again. Just hearing her given name on his lips had calmed and disarmed her, even more so than his earnestly frantic apologies and explanations.

"You slept in," he said, lightly rubbing her hand between his. "You must have needed it, after what you went through last night."

"I guess." She slid her hand free and ran it through her sleep-tousled hair.

A shadow passed over his face, just fleetingly, before he gestured her to the other stool. "Coffee? I've got a fresh pot."

"Definitely. Absolutely. Black, please."

"I can have a plate of eggs and bacon in front of you in five minutes."

"Can you make it four? I'm famished."

He gave her a swift once-over as he poured her coffee. "They'd sell a lot more of those pajamas if they had you modeling them. Men would buy them for their wives and girlfriends instead of black lace lingerie."

"Yeah, right." She accepted the steaming mug and took a tentative sip. She was a real hot ticket, all right, in these oversize, wrinkled jammies, with her hair all over the place and not a molecule of makeup. "You've got kind of a different look going there, yourself."

"My civvies." He hefted an iron skillet off the overhead rack and set it on the cooktop that occupied the other half of the island. Sorting through the contents of his refrigerator, he said, "I guess you've never seen me in anything but my professional monkey suits."

Or elements thereof. For awhile last night, after he'd given her his shirt and brought her upstairs, he'd been in nothing but his dinner trousers, with the suspenders dangling. He'd seemed completely oblivious to his state of undress, so preoccupied was he in making her comfortable and tending to her needs. At first, she was oblivious, too. But as the sherry warmed her and the nightmare receded, she became inexorably aware that he was naked from the waist up.

She'd known he was well-proportioned—long limbed and lean hipped, with broad, squared-off shoulders. And she'd suspected he was in good shape, having noticed his weight bench in a corner of the foyer. But she hadn't put it all together in her mind—hadn't envisioned the hard-packed muscles shaping a classically defined male torso. And she hadn't, for some reason, expected the mat of dark, velvety hair that blanketed his upper chest, tapering off somewhere below the waistband of his trousers.

She remembered stealing glimpses of him as they sat sideways on the Barcelona chair, David plucking bobby pins and bits of leaves from her hair while she, wrapped in a blanket, sipped her sherry. By sliding her eyes to the right, she could see them both in the glass over that wall of pictures. So intent was his concentration that he might have been disarming a nuclear warhead.

They looked like lovers, she'd realized, basking in the gentle tugging of his fingers and the comb, as soothing as a scalp massage.

"The police called this morning." Facing her across the island, David laid strips of bacon in the frying pan, arranging them just so with a pair of tongs. "Seems two men with puncture wounds to the face and torso showed up at Columbia-Presbyterian's emergency room around four o'clock this morning. Apparently they'd tried to self-medicate for pain with massive doses of something called...Sudden Comfort?"

"Southern Comfort," she said. "A popular general anesthesia in these here parts."

"It evidently didn't work very well, because by the time they'd made it to the E.R., they were—how did the officer put it?—howling and gibbering and screaming for pills."

"Was it them?" Nora asked.

"Yes, and you'll be pleased to know they've been taken up. Arrested. When the police questioned them, they admitted not only to the attack on you, but to a whole slew of other offenses, everything from forcible rape to armed robbery to—" Muttering a curse, David set the tongs down, gripped the edge of the work island and lowered his head. He let out a long, ragged sigh.

"David?"

He looked up and met her gaze, looking as stricken as he had last night when he first came downstairs and saw her. "Nora..." He shook his head. "It really was my fault, what happened to you. I drove you out there."

"You already apologized, David."

"I need to do it in the light of day. I'm sorry, Nora. When I think what they could have done to you—" He dragged a hand through his hair. "I've never felt so deeply ashamed. My actions last night were inexcusable. I think, deep down, I wanted to believe you were offering yourself to me simply because I..." He drew in a deep breath, meeting her gaze squarely. "I wanted you so much," he said softly. "That's the reason, but it's not an excuse. That's it, that's all I have to say. I'm sorry, and there's no excuse."

She nodded slowly. "I understand now what you thought was going on, and after all, I didn't exactly discourage you, not at first. We were both...under certain illusions. If I'd only given the situation a little more thought..." She rolled her eyes. "If I only hadn't gone into that damn park! That was *my* poor judgment, not yours."

"You can't be faulted for that." He picked up the tongs and turned the bacon, which was beginning to sizzle appetizingly. "What do Ohio farm girls know about such things?"

Nora stilled in the act of raising her coffee cup to her lips. "How did you know...?"

"You mentioned it last night. I guess you were too traumatized to remember. You kept saying you wanted to go home to your parents' farm. What kind of a farm is it?"

She took a pensive sip of her coffee. "Dairy."

"Really. I lived on a dairy farm of sorts in Tibet, but it was yaks I used to have to get up and milk, not cows.

Hardest I've ever worked in my life. How did you end up signing with Boss and moving to Milan?"

He'd never asked her about herself before, and she'd hated it. Now he was asking too much.

She licked her lips nervously, weighing the need for some credible fabrication against her loathing for subterfuge—especially given their newfound harmony. As thrilled as she was to have scored commissions from both Van Aucken sisters last night, she couldn't bask in that achievement, knowing she had to pretend to David—and to the Van Auckens and everyone else, of course—that it was her phantom friend who was the jeweler, and not she.

"Forgive me for prying," he said. "Here you've just awakened from one of the worst nightmares a woman can endure, and I'm interrogating you. You don't have to talk." With a wry smile, he added, "Not that I mind if you do."

They did talk as she was devouring her breakfast, but she steered the conversation away from herself and toward safe, impersonal subjects of general interest. As she was wiping up the last of her fried egg with her final bite of toast, it occurred to her that David, sitting on the stool next to her nursing a cup of coffee, hadn't had a cigarette yet.

"You usually smoke when you're drinking coffee," she observed. "Is it too much to hope that you're trying to quit?"

"As a matter of fact, I am."

"Seriously?" She pushed her plate away, drained the last of her orange juice. "Wow. What finally wised you up?"

He smiled a little self-consciously. "Your policy of not kissing men who smoke."

She just stared at him, her cheeks slowly heating.

"Don't worry," he said. "I promised you you'd be safe from unwanted attention, and it's a promise I intend to keep. That is…" He turned toward her on his stool, resting his elbows on his thighs, observing her with those midnight eyes. "Please tell me you'll keep seeing me. I know, after last night, you must have mixed feelings at best, but—"

"I'll keep seeing you," she said, thinking how odd it sounded to say it that way, as if they had really been involved and not just going through the motions.

Quietly he said, "I won't force my attentions on you, but you should know that, unless you ask me not to, I do mean to kiss you at some point. Not right away. I'll heroically resist the urge until you've had a chance to get over what happened to you last night, whether it takes days or weeks. But I think it's only fair to warn you of my intentions."

The very gravity of the little speech made it almost laughable, but Nora didn't so much as smile. "Do you mean you just want to kiss me, or…something more?"

A hint of amusement tugged at one corner of his mouth. "It's been my experience that kissing often leads to something more."

"I don't doubt that's been your experience," she said, recalling the helplessness with which she'd surrendered to his touch last night, even in the absence of any kissing. "The thing is…it hasn't been mine."

His eyebrows drew together.

"I'm a virgin, David."

Now it was his turn to stare, the skepticism in his eyes gradually transforming into plain old amazement.

"It's all right," she said, looking away and picking up her cup. "You can laugh if you want."

Softly, soberly, he said, "Why would I want to laugh?"

She swallowed some coffee, avoiding his gaze. "You know. Twenty-two and never been..." She shrugged.

"Nora." He took the cup from her and set it down, clasped her hands between his. "It's not your age—you're young, for heaven's sake, very young. It's just...well, I am a little surprised, given...I don't know...your profession, I suppose. The crowd you must run with and all—despite your assertions to the contrary. And you're just so...beautiful, so desirable. When you walk into a room, every man there follows you with his eyes. You can't tell me men haven't tried to..."

"I've had a hard time letting men get close to me, so I've just never been in the kind of relationship that might lead to...you know, where I might fall in love. And I always thought the first time...it should be with someone I love."

"Ah." David released her hands, looking a little perplexed. "Then last night, before...well, before I ruined everything, when we were...when you and I..." He rasped a hand over his beard-darkened chin. "I had just naturally assumed you intended to..."

"Sleep with you? Actually, I did, yes. Not because I'm in love with you," she added quickly, trying for some measure of cool. "Because, well, I'm not. No offense."

He gallantly inclined his head. "None taken."

"But I got to thinking that maybe I was being...too discriminating. If I was going to be that picky, I'd be a virgin forever."

"All right, I'll probably start taking offense fairly soon."

"You know what I mean."

He smiled. "I think I do, yes. You made an impulsive

All of Me

decision last night not to wait for love. May I take that as a sign that I haven't lost my touch?"

"That," she conceded, "and I thought you must have felt something for me—some glimmer of...*something*. When I realized you didn't..." She shook her head and turned away, embarrassed.

Out of the corner of her eye, she sensed him struggling for words.

"It was my own fault," she said, bailing him out. "I had it right originally. I *should* wait till I'm in love—which is probably never gonna happen, the way I am with men, but I'm gonna wait anyway. You probably think that's silly and childish—"

"On the contrary, I admire it. I respect it. Why shouldn't you hold out for true love? It means you want the best for yourself, and what's wrong with that? And if you hold your virginity in high regard, well, it's considered a precious commodity in most cultures. It *is* precious, when you think about it. It represents your innocence, your purity. It's the most priceless gift a woman can give a man. You should give it to the right man, Nora, and I'll probably kick myself later for saying this, but..." He sighed and shook his head. "I'm not the right man. You'd be sorry afterward."

"It's almost like you're saying you don't want to ruin me."

"Something like that. Make no mistake—I want you. Badly. You're that most rare and exotic of finds," he said, reaching out to graze her cheek with his knuckles, "an untouched woman. That only enhances your allure, which was pretty powerful already. But I'm not about to take advantage of you, and that's what it would amount to, especially given that...you don't have those kinds of feelings for me."

"Anyone ever tell you you were born in the wrong century?"

He chuckled. "Oh, I don't think there can be any doubt about that."

"So, uh...does this mean you're gonna go back to smoking?"

With seemingly genuine bewilderment he said, "Why would I do that, when it would keep you from kissing me?"

"Okay...didn't you just say we're not gonna, um..."

"That doesn't mean we can't kiss. It doesn't *have* to lead to...something more." He smiled.

She didn't return the smile. "Why do you want to kiss me, David?"

He looked nonplussed, as if this response were the last one he would have anticipated.

She said, "I mean, we've agreed that we don't harbor real feelings for each other." More or less. And it was pretty much untrue as regarded her; her feelings toward David might have been conflicted, but they were all too real. "Is it just...a physical thing?"

He appeared to be choosing his words carefully. "If it were, would you still let me kiss you?"

She bit her lip; he shifted his gaze to her mouth. "If you'd be satisfied with just kissing," she said.

"Of course I wouldn't. But if anyone can summon up the necessary self-restraint, I can."

"Think pretty highly of yourself, do you?"

"Hey, I *am* the Lord High Control Freak of the Universe," he said with a grin. "Or hadn't you heard?"

9

"YOU KNOW WHAT IT LOOKS like in here?" Nora asked, peering up at the chandeliers hanging from the fancifully decorated ceiling of Tavern on the Green's spectacular Crystal Room. "The inside of a wedding cake."

"The *inside* of a wedding cake." Smiling indulgently, David signaled their waiter for the check.

"Well, I mean, I know, in real life the inside of a wedding cake is, like...cake. But check this out," she said, her gaze sweeping the rococo confection of a dining room. "If wedding cakes looked on the inside the way they look on the outside," she said, "this is *exactly* what they'd look like."

"Has anyone ever told you you've got a rather singular outlook on things?" he asked, smiling at her over the top of his coffee cup.

She thought about it. "No. Just you."

He'd told her the same thing—or variations on it—more than once recently. He seemed to find her quirky, which pleased her. In art school, she'd been the straight one. High time someone noticed her "singular outlook."

Two weeks had passed since the MoMA benefit and the attack on her in the park, during which David had escorted her to several charity functions, including a luncheon here at Tavern on the Green last week to benefit the Kidney Foundation. The Crystal Room's frothy splendor had captivated the little girl in her from the moment she'd set foot in it.

Equally enchanting was the so-called Crystal Garden, visible through the glass walls that surrounded the dining room, in which the trees had been densely wrapped in strings of tiny lights, highlighting the wonderfully organic contours of every trunk, branch and twig. The first time David had taken her here, he'd commented that the light-festooned trees reminded him of her—nature rendered sublime.

"I love this place," she said.

"So I gather."

"Is that why you brought me back here tonight?" They had spent the early part of the evening in the grand and gilded ballroom of the Plaza Hotel, attending a fashion show to benefit breast cancer awareness. Afterward, instead of bringing her straight home, David had suggested a late supper here—the first time he'd taken her anywhere when it wasn't business for him.

He reached inside his suit jacket in search of the cigarettes that were no longer there, a habitual gesture with him lately, and the only outward indication that it was any challenge whatsoever to give up smoking.

Nicotine withdrawal wasn't the only thing he'd kept a stiff upper lip about lately. Not once in the past two weeks had he attempted to kiss her. Had he decided that it was a bad idea, after all?

"I brought you here," David said, "because I was feeling a bit peckish, and I thought you could use a bite, too."

"No, but why *here?*" She propped her elbows on the table to confront him squarely. They could have eaten at the Plaza, or a hundred other places. In fact, although David dined frequently at Tavern on the Green, its location on the western edge of Central Park just five blocks from his house making it ideal for entertaining clients, he'd told her that when it came to famously fabulous restaurants, he preferred the hushed contemporary polish of the Four Seasons. "I thought you said this place was a bit too 'intricately gorgeous' for your taste."

"It's growing on me."

That was probably as close as he was going to come to admitting he'd chosen this restaurant tonight simply to please her. As amicable as he'd been that morning in his apartment, and during the two weeks since, Nora sensed a certain lingering reserve on his part, a subtle guardedness.

She recalled how she'd worried, after he'd questioned her about her Ohio roots, that he would start digging into her background. She needn't have troubled herself. Other than one or two casual and baffling personal revelations—he'd seriously milked *yaks* in *Tibet?*—he'd volunteered little about himself and hadn't pressed her for details of her past. Eager as she was to demystify the enigmatic David Waite, she'd resisted the urge to delve into his history, knowing he would take that as his cue to do the same to her. Better to talk about movies, books, plays, politics, religion, the weather—*anything* but themselves. On that, they seemed to be in tacit agreement.

The waiter handed David a small leather folio, into which he tucked several large bills before handing it back. "Thank you, George. Keep the change."

"Thank *you*, Mr. Waite."

Rising, David said, "Shall we?"

Heads turned as they wove their way among the tables toward the exit, the women sizing David up with sideways glances, the men a little more obvious in their appraisal of Nora. The two of them looked like the ultimate, well-matched Beautiful Couple tonight, David in a flaw-

lessly tailored suit and silver tie and Nora in a cocktail
dress of, coincidentally, the same blue-black as his suit.

Of the six dresses Kevin had set aside for her before
leaving on vacation, she had left this one for last, because
it couldn't be worn with a bra, or even stockings. It was
two dresses, actually: a strapless tube of gleaming spandex that hugged her from breasts to upper thighs, and
over it a long-sleeved, tea-length gown of gossamer-
sheer silk that drifted and rippled like water. A matching
boa made of big, squiggly loops of satin ribbon com-
pleted the ensemble. Having wearied of putting her hair
up, she wore it loose tonight; David had found excuses to
touch it several times.

Although she felt a tad self-conscious without a bra,
she had to admit this outfit had been the perfect backdrop for her long gold chain with the pendant of dangling fire opals, crafted to resemble a cluster of grapes on
a vine. The piece had garnered a great deal of interest at
the fashion show and earned her—or rather, her
"friend"—two new commissions.

Of course, she couldn't fulfill those commissions until
she'd finished the pieces the Van Aucken sisters had ordered—four necklaces, four pairs of earrings, five bracelets and three rings altogether—which would take her
several more weeks to complete but earn her a hefty
profit and invaluable exposure. The only fly in the oint-
ment was, of course, having to keep her burgeoning business enterprise a secret from David. The more time they
spent together, the more uneasy it made her to be living a
lie this way. She consoled herself that he didn't really
want to know about her, that he didn't even really care
that much about her—he'd virtually told her that in so
many words.

Hadn't he?

Half an hour later, after catching every red light between Central Park West and Chelsea, David escorted
Nora into Harlan's building, grimacing as he approached
the elevator. He hated "lifts" in general, he'd once told
her, but especially lifts that were seventy years overdue
for an inspection.

Tonight, as always, he would walk her to the apartment door, say good-night after she'd unlocked it, and
leave, after which Nora would nuke herself a cup of hot
chocolate, go to bed and gaze up at the high, darkened
ceiling, wondering if and when he intended to kiss her.
The anticipation, which had felt exhilarating in the beginning, was swiftly morphing into plain old frustration.

If he'd changed his mind, he really shouldn't leave her
hanging like this.

Or...was he waiting for her to give him some sort of
signal? *I'll heroically resist the urge until you've had a chance
to get over what happened to you last night, whether it takes
days or weeks.*

He gestured Nora into the elevator, pulled the cor-
roded metal door and iron gate shut, and pushed the button for the sixth floor. Shoving his hands in the pockets of
his topcoat, he maintained his usual brooding, elevator-
loathing silence as the machine began its slow, rattling
ascent.

"So, uh..." Nora hugged the boa around herself, her
fist tightening on the handle of her little purse. "Harlan
and Kevin are coming back tomorrow."

"Yes?" David squinted overhead, as if by concentrat-
ing hard enough he could see right through the roof of
the elevator to inspect the status of the cables.

"I'm glad," she said, "'cause that's an awfully big
apartment for one person. Kind of creeps me out sometimes. Just 'cause it's so huge and filled with all this

weird stuff, not 'cause I'm nervous in general." *Shut up.* "It doesn't have anything to do with, you know, what happened in the park."

David turned to look at her.

Shut up. You're being too obvious. Shut up now and salvage your dignity.

"'Cause I'm over that." She looked down and fiddled with the clasp on her purse. "Totally. I mean, it was awful when it happened, but I wasn't really hurt that badly, and they caught those—"

He gripped her head with both hands, lifted her face and closed his mouth over hers, hard.

Her purse and boa slid to the floor. She wrapped her arms around him and returned the kiss, so deep she felt as if she were drowning, so rough it almost hurt.

He crushed her against the elevator wall, buried his hands in her hair, moaned deep in his throat....

Nora felt the elevator shudder to a stop at the sixth floor. Still he didn't release her, just went on kissing her, softer now, a caress of his lips against hers, light sweeps of his tongue between tremulous breaths, his hands moving now in her hair, the buttons on his coat digging into her chest....

It went on and on, drunkenly, this sweetly frantic, deliriously passionate kiss.

Just when Nora thought her heart might burst because it was so much, too much, he drew back a bit, breathless, and rested his forehead against hers.

They stood that way for a long moment, motionless, just getting their bearings.

"The elevator stopped," she said inanely.

He kissed her forehead. "Invite me in for a drink."

She bit her lip. "Just a drink?"

"I do plan on finding an excuse to kiss you again."

She chuckled. "All right, then. Would you like to come in for a drink?"

"I'd love to. Thanks for asking."

It was an hour before he kissed her again. They shared a glass of wine in the living room, and then David asked to see Harlan's notorious Warehouse of the Bizarre and Preposterous, which had evidently become something of a legend in the circles they ran in. The tour—during which she kept him well away from her jewelry-making station—concluded in her little dress-rack-enclosed nest. Impressed with the view, David raised all the window shades to expose as much as possible of the glittering skyline, then turned off the lights so they could curl up in the dark on her pillow-heaped daybed and gaze out at it.

He had her tucked into his embrace, her head against his chest. In the luminous semidarkness, she could see his hand as he lightly stroked her hair, rubbing strands of it between his long fingers as if testing its silkiness. They had both kicked off their shoes; David had also divested himself of his suit jacket and loosened his tie.

"I like your hair down like this," he said, and kissed the top of her head.

She craned her neck to look up at him. He smiled into her eyes, leaned down and touched his lips lightly to hers.

It was a gentle kiss this time, or at least it started off that way, mesmerizingly slow and soft.

He lay back against the pillows, easing her down on top of him as he stroked her hair, her arms, traced soft, circular patterns on her back....

She stiffened when he glided his hands lower, over the silk-clad curve of her bottom.

"Just let me touch you," he murmured. "Through your clothes."

She glanced anxiously toward the windows.

"No one can see us." He caressed her all over, lightly, as he kissed her. The sensation was hypnotic, making her feel both transported out of her skin and very much in it, a slave to his gradually deepening kisses, his ever more restless touch.

He tilted her head up, pressed his lips to her throat, over and over. She gasped when he probed her ear with the tip of his tongue, a sexual tremor coursing through her.

He closed his hands over her bottom, pulled her to him. Through the layers of clothes between them, she could feel how hard he was. He flexed his hips, pushing against her, a gesture so patently carnal that she gasped. "David..."

"Trust me." Tightening his arms around her, he flipped them over so that it was she who reclined on her back, with him on top, pressing her into the mound of pillows.

He took her mouth again, moving against her in a slow, sinuous rhythm, the rhythm of sex.

Desire thrummed through her. It felt so right, being with him like this, so natural. The temptation to answer his body's sensual dance with her own was nearly too powerful to resist. But resist it she did, wresting her head to the side and pushing against him. "You said you wouldn't..."

"I'm not going to."

"This is more than kissing."

He rolled off her and levered himself up on an elbow. "You've kissed men before, I'm sure."

"Yeah, of course."

"Much as I'd like to believe I'm first man to

ever...touch you the way I'm touching you, do the things
I'm doing, that's probably wishful thinking, isn't it?"

"'Fraid so," she admitted. "I'm a virgin, not a nun."

"Impudent wench." He smoothed her disheveled hair
off her face. "Did it trouble you as much then as it does
now?"

"It...didn't feel like this."

He smiled wolfishly. "Can I take that as a compli-
ment?"

"It's just that it doesn't seem like you intend to stop."
Not that she truly wanted him to. She ached for him, for
this; she'd wanted it forever. But not in the absence of
love.

"I'm not trying to seduce you, Nora, but I won't lie to
you. I want as much of you as you're willing to give. I
won't press the issue, because I did promise I would only
kiss you, and there's just so far I can stretch the definition
of that, but...there *are* things we can do for each other,
ways we can enjoy each other—" he trailed a hand over
her breast to her lower belly "—short of actually having
sex. I'd like to give you that kind of pleasure."

She shook her head. "David..."

"Let me," he murmured, caressing her through her
double-layered dress. "I want to take you all the way.
You don't have to do anything for me."

"No, David." Nora closed a hand over his; he stilled. "I
want to save that, too, for when it means something,
when it's a part of something..." She sighed and looked
away.

"For when you're in love," he said quietly, smoothing
errant strands of hair off her face.

"You think that's stupid," she said. "Infantile."

"No, I respect it," he said, adding ruefully, "but I don't
have to like it."

"We probably shouldn't be here like this," she said, hearing the ambivalence in her voice and suspecting David did, too.

"But I want to be here," he said, settling back onto her, their hips snugged together, legs entwined. "And I think you do, too. I can draw the line wherever you need me to, Nora. I assume you don't want me to touch you under your clothes."

She nodded. *I want you to rip them from my body.*

"And I know you want to stop short of...complete gratification. I can handle that." He lifted the pendant resting between her breasts and jiggled it, rattling the fire opals. "It'll be like reliving my adolescence, when I was only allowed to go so far."

"I assume you remember how frustrating that was," she said drolly.

"Deliciously frustrating, in a way," he said, teasing her left nipple by dragging the cluster of opals back and forth across it until it stiffened beneath the spandex fabric. "There's a certain piquant thrill in maintaining a state of unendurable arousal with no relief in sight. The pleasures of sexual restraint are highly underrated."

"This isn't smart, David. It would be too easy for things to get out of hand."

"You don't trust me to rein myself in," he said, sounding slightly affronted.

"It's not a matter of trust."

"Ah, but it is. I'm much stronger than you." Dropping the pendant, he seized her wrists, pinning them in the pillows. With one swift movement of his leg, he wedged her thighs apart and thrust between them. "I could force you, if I were so inclined. Deep down inside, you think I'm capable of taking you against your will."

His eyes glittered darkly as they searched hers; his

hands felt like iron vises around her wrists. Willing steadiness into her voice, she said, "I just think you might find it hard to stop if things get too...close to the edge."

With a look of resolve, David sat up and straddled her, gripping both of her wrists in one hand and using the other to tug open the knot of his silvery necktie.

"W-what are you doing?" she asked as he whipped the tie off and wrapped it securely around her wrists.

"Showing you just how close to the edge things can get, how far I can take you—and me—and still manage to stop, all on my own." Lifting her hands above her head, he lashed them to a cast-iron rung of the daybed, and smiled. "Even if you beg me not to."

"HAVE YOU EVER READ the *Kama Sutra?*" David asked as he bound Nora's right foot to a corner rung of the daybed, using a sequined belt he'd liberated from the dress rack behind him.

"You've probably read it cover to cover—in the original Sanskrit, no doubt." A sort of cocky acceptance had replaced Nora's initial alarm; she was brazening it out. Good.

"No, it was in English," he said, although in truth, the ancient classic of Indian erotica had been read *to* him, over a period of weeks, in bed, by the accommodating young widow from whom he'd rented his flat in Bombay. "It was Richard Burton's translation."

"*Richard Burton* knew Sanskrit?"

"*Sir* Richard Burton, the nineteenth-century explorer. He was a remarkable man—adventurer, linguist, anthropologist.... He's the closest thing I've got to an idol." David tested the give in the belt; just enough so she could bend her knee, without affording her the leeway to resist him or throw him off.

She tugged on her hand restraints, licked her lips; ah, so she *was* a little nervous. "Isn't the *Kama Sutra* all about...kinky positions and techniques and all that?"

"Actually, it's far more complex and sophisticated than most Westerners realize—quite a scholarly treatise on sexual passion in all its diversity and subtlety." He chose another belt off the rack, this one of gold leather, and snapped it.

She flinched.

"Some of the positions it describes are...inventive." He used the gold belt to secure her left foot to a bottom rung so that it was as far from her right as could be managed on the narrow daybed. His favorite of the *Kama Sutra*'s sexual variations had been the rather challenging position of *indrani*, but Kamala's legs had been so sore afterward that she'd only consented to it the once. "The main emphasis is on the techniques for exciting your partner's desire—what the author, Vatsyayana, called the 'Sixty-four Ways.'"

Mockingly Nora said, "Just sixty-four?"

"I know," he replied dryly as he stood to assess his handiwork. "I myself have catalogued nearly a thousand."

Never in his life had David seen anything more captivating than Nora Armstrong tied down hand and foot in that diaphanous gown, her hair tumbling over the pillows like a lustrous waterfall, looking up at him with that evocative mixture of compliance, defiance and trepidation. Did she think she was utterly in his power, or did she realize it was actually the reverse?

Nora's guilelessness, which had so enchanted him from the first, was not, after all, an act; she was a virgin, for pity's sake. The sensuality that infused her every word and gesture was, likewise, a real and intrinsic part of her. Her rather quaint resistance to his advances, and the heat he felt simmering just beneath it, conspired to hold him more firmly in her thrall than ever.

If the enchantment were merely sexual, he wouldn't be troubled. But there was an undercurrent of something deeper flowing between them, and that scared the hell out of him.

He'd resisted it, but to no avail. The trick now was to sustain their relationship—he'd rather slit his own throat than stop seeing her—but without stumbling into the treacherous pit of emotional involvement. It wasn't the fall he feared so much as the bamboo spikes at the bottom.

One could, on occasion, escape from the realm of the heart, but not without grievous wounds.

In truth, it was too late to avoid the pit completely; he'd been skidding down its rocky slope since that first night with her at the Waldorf. What he had to do now was climb out of that black hole of unwanted feelings and murky sentiment, without letting on that he'd ever fallen into it.

If Nora knew that he cared, even a little, what could have been a diverting acquaintance with a beautiful woman would degenerate into the dreaded Love Affair—and he'd had enough of that sort of thing to last a lifetime.

Sitting on the edge of the daybed, he stroked her face lightly with both hands, barely touching her. "There's a whole chapter in the *Kama Sutra* on the embrace, or more accurately, the art of touch." She closed her eyes as he prolonged the airy caress. When he moved on to her throat, she tilted her head back slightly, like a cat. She had a long, silken neck; he took his time gliding his fingertips over it, wishing they weren't quite so rough.

Trailing his fingers downward, he skimmed them over both breasts all the way to her hips, and back up again, and again, and again. The rise and fall of her chest increased a bit in tempo. Her nipples pushed against the elasticized bandeau dress she wore beneath that layer of

translucent silk. He let his fingertips brush them as they
passed, over and over, until they were hard as pebbles
and, if her spontaneous little shudders were any indication, highly sensitized.

Leaning over, he murmured against her lips, "There's
another whole chapter on the kiss."

She opened her eyes, enormous in the dark, and
looked right into him, in that unnervingly direct way she
had. He took her lower lip between his, teased it lightly
with his tongue, captured her helpless little sigh with his
mouth. Her eyelids drifted shut; so did his.

David framed her face with his hands as he kissed her,
taking his time about it, pleasuring her mouth with his.
He reveled in his heart when she kissed him back, her
languid passion a match for his own.

He lavished the same attention on her eyelids, her ears,
her throat, savoring her with his lips and tongue, nipping
her with his teeth, all the while caressing as much of her
as he could reach.

She went very still when he bent his head to her chest.
A soft little sound escaped her when he nuzzled a breast,
clearly unencumbered by a bra but bound all too snugly
for his liking. Sitting up, he raised the skirt of her sheer
overdress and glided both hands up beneath its bodice.

"David." Nora tensed. "You said you wouldn't—"

"Trust me." Taking hold of the top edge of the bandeau, David peeled it down over her breasts, then slid his
hands out and smoothed down the overdress. "See?
You're still covered."

In a manner of speaking. The flimsy gown revealed—
and enhanced—far more than it concealed. Nora's lush
breasts, thrust upward by the position of her arms,
strained against the gossamer silk, forming a voluptuous
niche for that exquisite opal pendant. Her nipples looked

enticingly dark, almost violet, through the inky-blue film, the flesh of her breasts milky white.

David ached, physically, just looking at her. Leaning down, he took first one nipple and then the other in his mouth while caressing both warm, weighty breasts through the liquid layer of silk.

Excruciatingly hard already, he cautioned himself to take this slowly. Tonight was about the journey, not the destination. This was his effort to earn Nora's trust, to prove that he could pull back, no matter how far things went.

He just hoped that he would be able to stop before his desire became ungovernable.

Forsaking her breasts for now, he trailed kisses down her belly, pausing at the juncture of her thighs. He could hear her breathing grow almost frantic, as she wondered what he would do.

That particular pleasure could wait, he decided. *Take your time....* Raising her right leg, exposed by her hitched-up dress, he pressed his lips to the soft inner part of her thigh just below the bottom edge of the bandeau. She fidgeted against her bonds as he rained light kisses up and down both legs, holding them still for this amorous assault. Her sweetly flustered response only stoked his hunger.

"One of the chapters," he said, the breathlessness in his own voice betraying his fierce state of arousal, "describes the various ways you can scratch your lover to heighten her pleasure."

"Scratch?"

Giving her no time to raise objections, David drew the nails of one hand up her left calf, grazing the tender underpart of the knee, which made her shiver, and all along her thigh. She sighed deliciously as he did the same to the other leg.

"The next chapter," he said, bracing himself over her, "is on biting."

"David..." she began, only to suck in her breath when he leaned down and closed his teeth over her throat, not as gently as he might have, but not hard enough to break the skin. She said nothing; her breathing, and his, were the only sounds to be heard.

Releasing her, he whispered, "Just trust me," and kissed the livid mark he'd left on her throat. Shifting downward, he lightly bit her shoulder and the upper swell of a breast. Finally he took a nipple between his teeth and tugged, scraping the ultrasensitive nub ever so lightly. He soothed the sting with a healing lick, which caused her to let out her pent-up breath in the form of a soft moan.

Raising his head to look at her, he said, "There's even a chapter on the different forms of striking."

Her eyes, languorous with desire, widened in alarm.

"It's all very ritualized," he assured her, rising over her to gauge her reaction to this prospect. "And as often as not, the man is the recipient of the blows. That wouldn't be the case this time, of course."

Her throat moved as she swallowed. "David..."

"You don't care for the idea."

"No."

He reached toward her face; she winced. Lightly stroking her cheek, he smiled. "It's not quite my cup of tea, either."

Realizing he'd been toying with her, she glared at him, but a little laugh forced its way through her outrage. "Bastard."

"There *is* one chapter I really rather like, though." He

rose off of her and shifted to the foot of the bed. "The one about pleasuring your lover with your mouth."

Gripping the hem of the bandeau dress, he tugged it up over her hips, so that the entire garment was now banded around her middle, rather like one of those waist cinchers Helena liked to incorporate in her Victorian-style evening gowns; he'd especially liked them.

He pushed the silken gown up to her waist as well, then sat back on his heels, drinking in the sight of her, bound and helpless in her sheer, disheveled gown and black satin thong. She yanked against the tie that bound her hands, her breasts heaving. He couldn't have imagined a more devastatingly erotic sight.

"David, you promised...."

"I promised not to bring you to climax." He rested a hand between her legs, finding her already wet; he could feel it through the satin. "I didn't say I wouldn't make you desperate for it."

Lowering his mouth to her, he paused, letting her feel the heat of his breath, drawing out the anticipation for both of them. Her entire body grew taut.

Nora let out a soft little cry at the first touch of his mouth where she was most inflamed. He nuzzled and kissed and licked her through the damp satin, gripping her hips to still her.

She murmured his name between ragged breaths, straining in her bonds as he pleasured her relentlessly, backing off from time to time to prolong the torment, but never stopping completely.

Her hips arched upward, trembling; he knew she was close.

As was he. So painfully aroused was he that all he could think of was yanking that flimsy little thong aside and hammering into her until he exploded, which would probably be instantaneous. She would be virginally tight, he thought, and wet....

Rising, he lowered himself onto her, molding his body to hers as she writhed, her eyes unfocused, her breathing harsh and shallow. He pressed against her, both of them quivering on the edge of release.

"David..." she moaned, "please..."

"Please stop?" He rubbed against her, caressing her breasts, knowing he was playing with fire but driven by an elemental hunger he could barely contain. "Or please go on?"

She answered him with a whimper, thrusting against him as if she were no longer in command of her actions. Even in the ambient half-light, he could see her pained expression—desire warring with reason—as well as a dark, telling flush of sexual excitement.

On the verge of climax himself, his hands gripping her hair he squeezed his eyes shut, summoning the strength to back off, as he'd promised her he would do.

Rein it in. Earn her trust.

"I promised I'd stop," he said hoarsely. "I promised...."

She shook her head. "Maybe...maybe we shouldn't stop."

No, don't tempt me. Don't say that, he thought desperately, his entire body quivering with the need to push into her, to possess her, to claim her innocence for his own.

I always thought the first time...it should be with someone I love.

"Maybe I was wrong," she said, "Maybe—"

"No." Taking her face between his hands, his grip a little too hard, he forced her to look at him. "You'd hate me afterward."

"I...no, I could never—"

"You would. I would have failed you. I would have taken something you never meant to give me." He sank onto her, burying his face in her hair, which was slippery-cool and redolent of lavender. "I don't want you to hate me, Nora. I couldn't live with that. It would kill me."

He was shaking, he realized, the feelings he'd kept so carefully imprisoned rattling their cage, screaming for release.

"Untie me," she said quietly.

He did as she asked, wondering if he'd blown it completely. Would she be furious with him for his unmerciful little demonstration?

She sat up, rubbing her wrists.

"I'm an idiot," he said, clawing his hands through his hair as he sat with his back to her on the edge of the bed. "I shouldn't have done this. I was trying to make a point, but perhaps—"

"Come here." Gathering him in her arms, she eased him down until they were lying together in a comfortable, and comforting, embrace. "You did make your point. And I've got to tell you, if I thought you were the Lord High Control Freak before..."

He chuckled along with her, feeling his distress and self-doubt evaporate in the face of her unconditional acceptance of him.

"You're not an idiot," she murmured as she stroked his hair. "How could you say that? You're the most extraordinary man I've ever known. And I could never hate you—not in a million years. I don't care how that sounds, or if you don't want to hear it. It's true."

David closed his eyes against the slow spinning of his world as he slipped deeper, deeper, into that place from whence there was little chance of escape, that black pit, that perilous but oh-so-seductive realm of the heart.

11

A DOZEN Eleanor Roosevelts locked arms for a spirited cancan, part of a production number in Act Three of *Two Little Exes* that the *New York Times* had dubbed "giddily surreal."

David glanced around at the rapt young audience—all of whom had donated $500 apiece toward AIDS research for the privilege of being here tonight—and conceded that Harlan had been onto something with that business about wooing Generation Xers into the philanthropic fold. So pleased was David to have sold out this benefit performance that he'd already given Harlan the go-ahead to plan the Halloween event he'd been lobbying for—an all-night costume party in an old hotel up on the Hudson that was reputed to be haunted, with ticket proceeds going to the Children's Cancer Research Foundation.

Nora, sitting next to him on a rickety folding chair—dreadful seating, but better than the hard little benches occupied by the people in the first few rows—smiled that dazzling smile of hers at the antics of the actors onstage. She looked intriguingly Victorian tonight, in a modestly cut, plum-colored velvet dress that buttoned down the front, emphasizing her generous bosom and exceedingly slender waist. Her hair was scraped back into a chignon, highlighting exquisite dangling earrings of amethyst and beaten gold—more of her friend's handiwork, obviously.

She was excruciatingly beautiful, the most desirable woman he'd ever known; it was maddening to know he'd never have her, not completely. Their physical relationship, although nothing short of electrifying, was nevertheless destined to remain unconsummated. Three weeks ago, the night of his *Kama Sutra* demonstration, he had made certain promises—and proven he could keep them, in the face of the most extraordinary temptation, including her own surrender to it. As a result, she had trusted him enough since then to explore with him the sensuality she'd kept under wraps for so long—something of a double-edged sword.

On the one hand, he felt honored that she'd given him as much of herself as she had. On the other, he was more consumed than ever by sexual hunger, which tended, on occasion, to bring out a reckless aggression in him; the trick was to keep the beast fed and happy, but well chained. So far, he'd managed to do just that, but it wasn't always easy. He ached just thinking about "kissing" Nora, which was their euphemism for bringing each other to the maddening, breathless edge of climax.

He'd found that she liked to please him—a refreshing contrast to the chilly self-involvement of his recent women friends. With that in mind, during their most recent date he'd happened to mention his taste for old-fashioned ladies' underthings—corsets, bustiers, garter belts and the like. Not that he had anything against her tantalizing little thongs and thigh-high stockings, but there was something about tight lacings and whalebone and complicated little fasteners that sent his libido into overdrive.

When he'd picked her up tonight and found her done up like a fantasy version of a nineteenth-century schoolmarm, complete with tight, high-heeled lace-up boots be-

All of Me

low the long, swirling hem of her dress, he'd begun to entertain the hope that maybe, just maybe, she'd extended the fantasy to those parts of her attire that were hidden from view. All through dinner at Tavern on the Green, where they'd become regulars over the past few weeks, he'd silently speculated on what she might or might not be wearing underneath all that high-necked, long-sleeved velvet. It would be midnight or later, when the play and ensuing party were over and he could spirit her back to his apartment, before he could find out.

So preoccupied was he with these ruminations that he'd absorbed very little of the play, but then he'd seen it before, as had Nora. In fact, she'd seen it several times; that was what came of sharing digs with its wardrobe manager.

So surely she wouldn't mind missing the conclusion tonight.

Leaning toward her, he whispered, "Let's get out of here."

"Now?" He knew she was thinking about his responsibilities as the organizer of this event.

"Just for a bit." He smoothed his hand up and down her arm, letting it graze the side of her breast.

She looked around a little self-consciously, but no one was paying any attention to them, which was why he'd felt free to touch her that way in the first place. The only audience member who seemed less than completely entranced by the play was Alec Van Aucken, two rows up, who'd been carrying on a whispered flirtation with the redheaded Amazon next to him since the curtain opened.

"Come on." David took Nora's hand, stood and led her quietly out of the makeshift auditorium to the dismal, windowless space that served as the theater's lobby—magically transformed tonight by Harlan Armstrong into a rather impressive version of Mount Olympus, utilizing the Greek columns and statuary David had seen in Harlan's remarkable promptuary of props. Olive trees and laurel garlands—silk, presumably, and twinkling with fairy lights—disguised the unpainted brick walls. The air was filled with the savory aroma of rosemary-encrusted lamb kebabs, which a Greek chef was turning on electric grills.

"David! Nora!" Harlan, in midhuddle with a cluster of young Greek-costumed waiters, turned and waved his clipboard at them. "Where are you going? You're not leaving before the party, are you?"

"Just thought we'd stretch our legs," David said. "Perhaps do a bit of exploring. This looks like a pretty interesting old building."

Harlan frowned. "It's just a warehouse, or used to be. Nothing much to..." His gaze lit on Nora's hand in David's, for which David mentally kicked himself. This was why he normally disdained any public demonstrations of affection, why he avoided touching Nora or even returning her fond looks except when they were alone. He'd been brought up to keep his cards close to the chest, the reasoning being that one's private concerns were simply none of anyone else's business.

But David had slipped in the heat of the moment, so to speak, giving Harlan the opportunity to put two and two together. This was especially vexing in that Harlan was, at best, ambivalent about David's evolving relationship with Nora, despite having been the instrument of it. He was worried, Nora had confided, that David would break her heart. "Explore away," he said, and turned back to his toga-clad servers.

Beyond the backstage area, past a musty storage space filled with sets and props—where they stopped for a long, breathless kiss—they found what appeared to be a communal dressing room, empty at present, every actor in the production being required onstage for the big finale. Shoes and hats were strewn everywhere, but the costumes were all arranged neatly on rails. Against one wall, below a long mirror surrounded by lightbulbs, stood a counter scattered with makeup, hairdressing paraphernalia and wigs on stands. The room was dimly lit, the only source of light being the bulbs around the mirror.

Nora wandered over to the counter. David locked the door and followed her.

"Look at all this stuff." She trailed her hand through a shoebox filled with lipsticks, rattling them, her reflection luminous in the mirror. "Have you ever seen this many—" She broke off with a gasp when he reached around her and seized her breasts, squeezing them firmly as he nuzzled her neck.

"I've been hard all night," he murmured, pressing against her to prove it, "wondering what you've got on under this."

Nora met his reflected gaze in that forthright way she had, her mouth relaxing into a hint of a smile, and unbuttoned the dress to the waist.

He opened it, his breath leaving him in a sigh of carnal wistfulness. In lieu of a bra, she wore a stiffly contoured merry widow of black lace on cream satin, which thrust her bosom into ripe display, her nipples barely concealed; indeed, one deep breath and she would surely spill out of it altogether.

"I've never wanted you more." He captured her hands, flattening them on the counter in such a way that she was forced to bend forward over it. "I could take you right here," he murmured into her ear.

She looked up at him in the mirror, her gaze as direct as before, and with a hint of something else, her new-found sense of sexual power. David liked seeing that in her. He liked it that she knew she had the upper hand, regardless of how aggressive he got, how demanding his unappeased desire made him—which was as it should be. Women were meant to do the choosing; men waited to be chosen.

He straightened, smoothing his hands up her arms. She started to push herself up from the counter. "Not yet." He pressed her back down with one hand while whipping her skirt up with the other. "Ah."

The bottom half of the merry widow, while more substantial than her usual thongs, nevertheless revealed that delicious bottom to good advantage. Her black, seamed stockings connected to the provocative undergarment by means of garters. Adding a bit of bad-girl allure were those severe black boots, which laced all the way up to the knees.

For a moment, all he could do was stare. "I think my heart just stopped."

She chuckled as if pleased with herself.

"Impudent wench. You've deliberately enticed me, knowing I'm honor bound not to give you what you're asking for." Closing his hands around her hips, he thrust against her, thinking he really ought not to; he'd been aroused all night, and now he was on a hair trigger.

She grinned at him over her shoulder, cheekily thumbing her nose at his state of sexual turmoil. "You said you wanted me to wear something like this."

"I only told you I liked this sort of thing," he said, slipping a hand between her legs to caress her through the snug undergarment.

"I can take a hint." She arched her back like a cat as he

fondled her, affording him an astonishing view of her cleavage in the mirror.

"Can you die from sexual frustration?" he asked hoarsely.

"If so, I think what we've got going on between us amounts to a suicide pact." Her eyes grew unfocused, as they did when she was excited; a rosy stain began to rise from her chest to her throat.

David felt a seam in the lacy strip between her legs and discerned that it was made to open there by means of hooks and eyes. On impulse he flicked it open.

Nora bolted upright and turned to face him, her skirt fluttering back down. Her surprise showed on her face; he had promised to touch her only over her clothes, and so far he'd managed to keep that promise.

"David," she began, "if you're going to start... touching me like that, you have to know where it'll lead."

"Then *you* do it," he murmured, raising her skirt.

"Do what?"

"Touch yourself like that." Taking her hand, he steered it beneath her skirt, molding it between her thighs.

Her eyes widened, as if the request astounded her. She tried to wrest her hand away, but he pressed it more firmly to her, moving closer so that she was essentially trapped between him and the countertop.

Cupping her face with his free hand, he said softly, "I'd love to see you come apart that way, even if I'm not the one making it happen."

"We said we wouldn't...go that far."

"We said we wouldn't do it to each other. We never said we couldn't do it to ourselves."

She arched an eyebrow. "Don't you think you've already pushed the definition of *kissing* about as far as it can go?"

"Please, Nora." He kissed her, coaxing her hand in a gentle, self-pleasuring caress. "I lie awake at night, imagining what you look like when you come, how you move, what kinds of sounds you make."

He deepened the kiss—and the caress, guiding it to a bolder, more frankly sexual rhythm.

Breaking the kiss, she said, "David, please. I can't...I couldn't." She shook her head. "Not in front of you."

"Don't be self-conscious. It would be so beautiful, so exciting."

"No, David."

He stilled and met her gaze, which was serious, almost grave. There came a muffled roar of applause, punctuated by whoops of approval from the audience. It went on steadily for a bit, growing even louder and more hectic around the point the curtain calls would be commencing.

"I'm sorry," she said. "I want to please you, but—"

He silenced her with a kiss, releasing her hand to enfold her in his embrace. "You do please me. Immensely. Never doubt that." With a sigh, he added, "*I'm* sorry for pushing you as I did. It's just that I want you so desperately—as much of you as I can have. I'm too greedy."

"It's not greed to want what you want—what we both want. It's natural." She laid a hand against his cheek. "Maybe it's a bad idea, us generating all this heat without ever cooling it off. I mean, it's making me kind of crazy, too. Maybe we're pushing the envelope too hard. Maybe we ought to back off, not be so...physical."

The background cheering rose to a crescendo as he kissed the tip of her nose, smiled into her eyes. "Maybe you ought to stop questioning a good thing."

"Is it a good thing? I know you say you're willing to take what you can get, but don't you think maybe we're..." She looked toward the door as the knob began to jiggle; there came a muttered curse and the jingling of what could only be keys.

"Damn." David started hastily rebuttoning her dress from the waist up; she did the same from the neck down.

The door flew open; overhead strip lighting zapped on. Kevin stood there, scowling at them as they frantically shoved the last two buttons in their holes. "No sex in the dressing room. It's my number one rule."

"It's not what it looks like." David would have denied it even if they'd been going at it like minks, having been brought up to offer whatever gentlemanly lies were required to protect a lady's reputation.

In a mocking parody of David' accent—what *was* it about his manner of speech that these Americans found so uproarious?—Kevin said, "What it looks like, old man, is a shag-fest behind locked doors, which I normally regard as a smashing good idea, but which I simply will not tolerate in my dressing room."

Nora snorted. "Shag-fest?"

"And you thought I didn't have a romantic soul." Kevin stepped aside to allow entrance to a procession of cast members, all talking and laughing at once as they yanked off wigs and kicked off shoes. Most of them were sweat-drenched Eleanor Roosevelts, but there was also a Joan of Arc, a Harriet Tubman, and a verdigris-painted Statue of Liberty in foot-tall platform shoes and a gigantic spiked headdress.

Miss Liberty squeezed between David and Nora to snatch a tub of removing cream off the counter. "No nookie in the dressing room. Kevin will spank you."

"Mustn't have that." Taking Nora's hand, David led

her out of the dressing room and back to the lobby, where the audience was milling about with their skewers of lamb and glasses of wine, waiting for the cast to join them. On a small stage in one corner, musicians played a twangy Greek folk tune on bouzoukis and *baglamas.*

"David!" Alec, standing with his majestically tall, black-vinyl-clad redhead, waved them over with a lamb kebab. "Outstanding evening." He slapped David on the back.

"Yes, it's really coming up trumps."

"I'd like you to meet a brand-new friend of mine." Alec stroked the redhead's arm in a way that suggested they'd become very friendly very fast. "This is Tania. No last name—just Tania. And here we have Nora..." He grimaced in evident concentration. "Something to do with muscles..."

"Armstrong." Nora shook Tania's hand. "Nice to meet you."

"And this—" another backslap "—is my racquetball buddy, David Waite." Alec was in high spirits, a sure sign that he expected to have rogered this girl twice before the night was out.

David offered his hand to Tania. "How do you do?"

"I'm cool," she said. "Hey, listen, Alec just told me something that *so* blew me away. Did you guys know all those women in the play were, like, *men?*"

David nodded. "It was Snow White's baritone that did it."

"Tania's a model, too," Alec told Nora. "And an aspiring actress."

"I did a commercial," Tania told Nora, a little smugly. "Maybe you saw it. Free-Style Tampons?"

Nora blinked. "Um..."

"I'm doing cartwheels in this, like, skintight, shiny white one-piece leotard thingy. You must have seen it."

"Um..."

"It's on all the time. You'll see it. You do any acting?"

"Um, no, just modeling."

"What agency are you with?"

"Boss."

"Yeah? I'm with Elite. I'm getting forty-five hundred a day now. What about you?"

"Come here a sec." Alec grabbed David by the arm and pulled, calling, "We'll be right back, ladies." When they were out of earshot, he asked, "So where'd you two sneak off to?"

"We, uh, took a little walking tour and ended up in the dressing room."

"Yeah? The stage manager told me that's a no humping zone."

"Looking for a trysting place already? I had the impression you two had just met."

"Yeah, we did, but she became very eager to, uh, accelerate our acquaintance when I happened to mention that I work for NBC."

"As a lawyer. You don't have anything to do with casting decisions."

"I'd kind of appreciate it if you didn't mention that to her." Alec smiled knowingly at David as he took a bite of his kebab. "So, uh, you and Nora are pretty hot and heavy, huh?"

"We were just talking in the dressing room, nothing more."

"Is that how her buttons ended up like that?"

David looked toward Nora, nodding and smiling as Tania held forth. A button on the lower part of her bodice was misaligned; his fault. *Damn*.

Thinking about their frantic attempt to tidy her up reminded him that she'd never gotten that merry widow refastened. Knowing she was essentially sans underwear in the midst of this crowded gathering was oddly titillating. Hell, everything about her titillated him in one way or another. She was both the sexiest woman he'd ever known and the sweetest. Those two qualities should have been mutually exclusive, but they weren't.

"So, is it love?" Alec asked.

David sighed and grabbed a glass of wine off a passing waiter's tray. "It isn't like that. It's just...a good time while it lasts."

"Which has been what, like, six weeks so far? Isn't that something of a record for you? I mean, aside from Madame Helena." Alec shivered dramatically and rubbed his arms, as if an icy wind had just passed through the room.

David gulped his wine. "That doesn't mean anything."

"Come on—you're with her constantly, and I see the way you look at her."

Like mother, like son. Didn't the Van Auckens have anything better to do than take notes on his love life?

"You're crazy about her." Alec tossed his stripped-clean skewer on a tray of used wineglasses.

Eager to redirect the conversation, David said, "Does Patsy know about your—" he nodded toward Tania "—extracurricular activities, or does she think you're saving it all up for your wedding night with her?"

Alec snagged his own glass of wine. "Activities can only be *extra*curricular if there's a *curricular*. There's not going to be any wedding. Patsy and I are just—"

"Bullshit, Alec. I see the way *you* look at *her*—and hold her hand and laugh together and whisper in her ear. She doesn't know, does she?—about the other women. She really does think she's the one and only, that your love for her is pure and profound and that you're just waiting for the right moment to pop the question."

A rare spark of anger flashed in Alec's eyes. "What, exactly, makes this any of your business, David?"

"The fact that I'm your friend. I've got to warn you, Alec, if you continue to take Patsy for granted the way you do, some smarter bloke is going to steal her away from you."

Alec shrugged and nonchalantly scanned the room. "She's not mine to steal. If she finds someone, I'll be happy for her."

"You'll be devastated. She's the companion of your heart, your soul mate. You assume she's a constant, that she'll always be there because she's always been there, yours and yours alone. Your mother was right—you're spoiled rotten."

"Are you done yet, or is there anything else you'd like to add before I tell you to bite me?"

"Just that she's very pretty, in case you hadn't noticed, and a fine woman. When she gets tired of waiting for you, I'll lead the cheering, because frankly, she deserves better."

"You talk like I've been abusing her somehow."

"There's a reason she thinks you're in love with her, Alec. Either you've just been leading her on all these years, which would make you the worst sort of rotter, or you feel a lot more than you're admitting to yourself."

"Yeah, well..." Alec clapped him on the shoulder. "You should know about that, buddy." He turned and stalked away.

12

"GOOD LORD," David said, "is that Patsy Crane?"

"Which one?" Nora asked, scanning the throng of costumed revelers celebrating Halloween in the Tudor-style great hall of Gatwick Castle, this ostensibly haunted gothic-revival mansion-turned-hotel.

"The harem girl. She just came in."

Nora tracked his gaze to a petite young woman in an extremely revealing Arabian Nights getup comprised essentially of a minuscule gold bikini gussied up with pink chiffon and spangles. She was surveying the crowded room as if looking for someone.

"Her?" Nora squinted at the eyes above the half veil covering the woman's lower face. Even with all the exotically overdone eyeliner, she realized it was, indeed, Patsy. "Wow. That's...kind of a different look for her, isn't it?"

"Beryl's handiwork, no doubt—an effort to remake Patsy into the type of cartoon sex kitten her son can't seem to get enough of. I prefer my women a bit more three dimensional." David smiled at Nora in that intimate way that always sent hot shivers down her spine—especially since he was otherwise so reserved with her in public. The effect was all the more arresting because of his vampiric attire—a sweeping black cape over white tie and tails. The Dracula likeness was rendered particularly effective by his height, his coloring and that darkly penetrating gaze. Turning that gaze on her, he said, "My taste tends more toward the…pink cheeked and pastoral. Especially tonight."

Nora was Little Bo Peep tonight, courtesy of Kevin, who'd dug into his historical costumes and done her up as the quintessential romanticized shepherdess—right down to the ruffled pantaloons and petticoats peeking out from beneath her blue swagged skirt. Her white peasant blouse was cinched in by a black velvet, front-lacing stomacher and accessorized with a lacy scarf tied over her shoulders. But it was Kevin's attention to detail that had really pulled the look together: a flat straw hat secured over her two braids with a blue satin ribbon, high-heeled slippers with enormous buckles, and a tall, curved crook.

"I never thought I'd be entertaining fantasies about pantaloons," David said. "I need to get you alone. Soon."

With a self-satisfied smile, Nora turned her attention back to Patsy, now talking to Harlan and Kevin, both out-fitted in full-body sheep costumes that left nothing but their faces exposed. Harlan's clipboard only added to the surreal effect. In response to some question of Patsy's, Harlan pointed toward the arched doorway that led to the hotel's guest rooms. Every attendee had been pro-vided a room—Nora's and David's adjoined—although it was assumed that most of them would be partying in the great hall until dawn. Harlan had scheduled seances throughout the night, complete with ghostly special ef-fects, culminating in an appearance by the phantom of the railroad tycoon who'd built Gatwick Castle, only to hang himself in its attic the night he moved in.

After Patsy left, Harlan and Kevin came over and joined them. "Here we come," Kevin said, "wagging our tails behind us."

"Hey, did you guys see that woman I was talking to?" Harlan asked. "Was that Patsy Crane?"

"That's right," David said.

Harlan peered at his clipboard. "I thought she wasn't coming. I know I crossed her name off."

Nora shrugged. "She must have changed her mind."

"Where did she go?" David asked.

"Hmm?" Harlan frowned at the clipboard. "Oh, she was asking if I knew where Alec Van Aucken was, and I told her I saw him head off to his room a little while ago. Here it is!" He tapped the clipboard with his pen. "I *knew* I crossed her off."

"Was he alone?" David asked.

Harlan looked up. "Sorry?"

"Alec. Was he alone when he went to his room, or was there someone with him?"

"No, he had another guest with him, that blonde in the French maid outfit, the one with the..." He cupped a hand in the vicinity of his fleecy chest. "He said he wanted to show her a stain on the wallpaper that he thinks looks like a man hanging by his..." He winced and looked toward the arched doorway. "Shit."

Kevin scowled at him. "Don't you feel sheepish now?"

David gestured for Nora to follow him toward the doorway. "A woman's touch might prove helpful here."

They sprinted upstairs to the second-floor hallway, where they encountered Patsy coming toward them in tears. A door banged open and Alec Van Aucken, his pirate shirt untucked, lurched out on his fake peg leg, frantically rebuttoning his breeches with the hand that had not been replaced by a hook. "*Patsy!*" he screamed as he stumbled after her. "Honey, wait! Please! Let me explain!"

"You don't have to." Patsy ripped off her veil as she

turned to face him. The French maid stepped warily out of Alec's room, her little white mobcap askew, her crimson lipstick smeared. "People tried to tell me about you—about the women," Patsy said, "but I didn't want to believe them. I thought..." She shook her head, rubbing at the inky trails of her tears. "Obviously I was wrong."

"No! Please, Patsy, you weren't wrong," Alec declared as he limped toward her. "*I* was wrong, I was stupid, but—no, don't!"

Patsy yanked a ring off her right hand—a massive sapphire, from what Nora could see of it—and hurled it at Alec. It bounced off his wooden leg and rolled down the hall. "I don't ever want to see you again."

"You don't mean that, Patsy. Patsy, wait!" Alec cried as she turned and descended the stairs. "*Patsy!*" He hobbled after her, calling her name and begging her to come back.

David grabbed him. "Let her go, Alec."

"*No!*" Alec wailed, close to tears himself, it seemed. "You don't understand!"

"I do. You're going to have to let her go."

Turning toward the stairs, Nora said, "I'll go make sure she's okay." After a futile search of the interior of the hotel, Nora finally found Patsy sitting behind the wheel of her Saab in the darkened parking lot, clutching a sensible woolen coat over her harem outfit and sobbing hysterically.

Sliding into the passenger seat, she patted Patsy's shoulder and handed her tissue after tissue until her weeping had tapered off to a succession of sad little hiccups.

"It was Alec's m-mother who talked me into coming here," Patsy said as she gazed through the windshield at nothing. "'Surprise him,' she said. 'Show up unexpect-edly in something provocative.' Beryl said I n-needed to be sexier if I wanted Alec to—" she glanced awkwardly toward Patsy "—take the next step. I thought he l-loved me. He didn't, but...I was sure he intended to marry me—why would he have given me a ring like that if he didn't? But he never seemed to want to...you know."

"Did he ever...kiss you?"

"Yeah, but never like...well, like I'm sure David kisses you. But, see, that's the thing," she said, turning toward Nora. "I decided maybe it was my fault. I've always been afraid to be, you know—sexy. I'm not like you. You're just so n-naturally..."

Nora rolled her eyes. "You have no idea how terrified I am to draw that kind of attention to myself. Or...I used to be. I've changed." Her relationship with David had changed her, made her embrace the power that came with her femininity.

"I wanted to change, too," Patsy said. "I wanted Alec to want me as a *woman*. But what happened was I waited too long. I should have done this—thrown myself on him like this—years ago. There's a right moment for every-thing, and the right moment for me to do this passed a long time ago."

"But you just said he doesn't really love you. Would you still have wanted to make love to him, even if he didn't—"

"Oh, yes," Patsy said gravely. "Yes. He was the one—that's the important thing. I loved *him*, even if he didn't love me back. He should have been my first. Even if he didn't want *me*, all of me, I could have made him want part of me, for a while. And I could have had a part of him."

"Would that have been enough?"

"If it was all I could have had, I would have taken it. And maybe—who knows?—maybe if I *had* thrown myself on him, it might have shocked him into acknowledging his feelings for me. I think they were there at one time, just...hidden too deeply for him to get at." She drew in a deep, trembly breath. "But the right moment passed. Now I'll never know."

Shaken into silence, all Nora could do was stare at her.

"I'm twenty-seven years old," Patsy said, turning back to the windshield, "and a virgin, and for the rest of my life I'll be kicking myself for not letting him be the first. Whatever you do, Nora, don't ever let that moment pass."

After Patsy left, Nora went back inside and lurked in the entrance to the great hall, now lit only by candlelight, watching Harlan and the hotel staff organizing guests around tables for the first seance of the evening. It was a while before she saw David, watching this undertaking from the shadows of the arched doorway to the guest rooms, a seductive specter in his white tie and black cape.

I loved him, even if he didn't love me back. He should have been my first.

When had she fallen in love with David? Nora wondered. It didn't matter. She was in love with him. This aching pleasure just at the sight of him, this deep thrill whenever he was close, this yearning, this need, couldn't be anything but love.

I waited too long...I should have thrown myself on him....

He was experienced, Nora thought, and passionate, and...

And she loved him. She loved him.

I could have had a part of him...

From across the crowded hall, he caught her eye and smiled—that private, slightly mysterious smile that always undid her. He backed up in the darkened doorway, until all she could see of him was his hand, beckoning her to come upstairs with him.

Whatever you do, Nora, don't ever let that moment pass.

DAVID HAD NO SOONER locked the door of his room than he tossed Nora onto the big, comforter-draped brass bed and unceremoniously threw her skirts up. The result was a great chrysanthemum of petticoats with two long, pantalooned legs emerging from the center.

"How exceedingly convenient," he said, noting that the pantaloons had been fashioned with a split crotch, closed at present with a row of dainty little shell buttons. He grew instantly aroused, thinking about undoing those buttons one by one...which would never happen, of course, since he was obliged to resist the overpowering temptation to undress her.

Nora shoved her skirts back down and sat up. "My bonnet's getting crushed."

"We must remove it, then." He tugged loose the satin bow and flung the hat across the room like a Frisbee. "No need to stop there," he said, reaching for the lace tippet that had been hiding her magnificent bosom from view all night.

"Uh-uh." She squirmed away from him and got off the bed. Addressing him squarely, hands on hips, she said, "You have to lose an item of clothing for every one that I lose."

"Easily done." Standing up, he flung his cape off and swiftly removed her scarf. One by one, he traded his long black tail coat, white tie, stiff wing collar, white piqué waistcoat, braces, gold studs and sleevelinks for her skirt and multitudinous petticoats—which she stripped off and set aside with a lingering finesse that would have done Salome proud. By the time she was down to her pantaloons, blouse and that enticing little black velvet stomacher, he was stiff as a rod beneath his trousers.

Sitting on the edge of the bed, she kicked off one buckled slipper for each of his black patent shoes. "I guess that's it."

Parting her legs, he knelt on the carpeted floor between them. "Isn't there anything else I can talk you out of? I'll gladly get stark naked if it will help."

She lifted the two braids draped over her breasts, each secured with a narrow strip of lace. "I could lose these."

"Tease." David took her in his arms, kissing her deeply as he caressed her breasts through the handkerchief linen of her blouse, gratified to find that she wore no bra beneath it. He cupped the warm, resilient flesh, thumbed her nipples until they grew taut. "What I wouldn't give," he said, fingering the satin drawstring that gathered the neckline of her blouse, "to be able to untie this."

After a moment's pause, she said, "It's okay. You can."

He searched her eyes. Any sort of complete disrobing went against their understanding. Two weeks ago, she had protested when he'd unfastened her merry widow. Perhaps she didn't view above-the-waist nudity as being quite so fraught with peril.

She smiled reassuringly. "It's all right. Really."

He pulled on the drawstring, which came easily untied. The gathers relaxed immediately, the thin linen slipping off one shoulder, creamy in the warm light from the bedside lamp. Taking hold of the blouse, he loosened the remaining gathers and released it. She spilt into his hands, hot and heavy and soft and perfect, so perfect.

"You're so beautiful, Nora. Impossibly beautiful." Cradling her breasts in his hands, he kissed her, slowly and softly. When he lowered his head, she guided him with her hands, letting him know she wanted this, too. He lavished kisses on her silken flesh. Closing his mouth over a nipple, he suckled her rhythmically, massaging the stiff little bud with his tongue while her heartbeat, which he could feel through her left breast, quickened in time with his own.

He gripped her hips, pulling her forward so that they were snugged together, his rigid heat prodding her through their clothes. *If only...if only...*

"Make love to me, David."

He looked at her. She was serious.

After a moment's sober reflection, he kissed her softly, lifted her blouse back up to cover her and retied the drawstring. Gaining his feet, he joined her on the bed, pulling her into his arms as he settled back against the mound of eyelet-covered pillows heaped against the brass bedhead. He kissed her hair. "You don't really want that, Nora."

"I do." She glided a hand downward until it rested on the rock-hard ridge beneath his trousers. "And so do you."

She'd never touched him there, as if fearful of inciting him to the point where even he, with all his good intentions and backbone, couldn't stop. He moaned when she shaped his length with her fingers through the smooth wool.

He seized her hand, threaded his fingers together with hers. "You'd be sorry afterward. You'd regret not having saved yourself for a man who..." He hesitated, wondering why he couldn't say it.

"Who loves me?" She tilted her head to look up at him. "I've changed my mind."

"Once before you changed your mind," he pointed out. "Afterward, you were grateful that I was strong for both of us. If I weaken this time, you'll only despise me for it."

"No I won't. I don't want you to be strong tonight, David." She sat up and faced him, untying the lace ribbon that bound her left braid. "Don't you understand? I *want* to make you weak. I want to make you so crazy with desire that you completely forget to be the Lord High Control Freak for just one night. You always hold on so tight to those reins. Can't you ever drop them and let someone else take the lead?"

He stroked her face. "It's not in my makeup."

"Maybe I should do something about that." Lifting his hand from her cheek, she stretched it out to the side, closing it around the horizontal brass rod that formed the top of the bedhead.

"What are you—"

"You'll see." She wrapped the band of lace firmly around his wrist and tied it to the brass rod. Stunned, a little amused and in no small measure excited by this turn of events, he offered no resistance, even when she crossed to his other side and tethered his left hand as she had his right.

"What devilry have you got planned, then?" He gave his bonds an experimental tug, but they didn't budge. His heart speeded in response to being immobilized this way; his senses went on alert. Bondage had never been quite the turn-on for him that it was for some—except for the time he'd tied Nora down, which ranked as his most incendiary amorous exploit to date—but in the spirit of sexual adventure, he'd thrown a bit of it into the mix from time to time. It had always been the woman who'd submitted to the restraints, however; he'd balked at that role.

Now he knew how it felt. A low-level panic thrummed

in his veins, enhancing a dizzying frisson of erotic antic-ipation.

"There's no footboard on this bed, nothing to tie your feet to." Straddling him, she opened his shirt and combed her fingers through his chest hair. "I'll just have to hold you down as best I can."

"Nora, this isn't smart. For one thing, we haven't got any sort of...protection."

That seemed to take the air out of her. "You don't have any condoms in your wallet?"

"I didn't think I'd be needing them. Not that there's any...well, any health risk. I've always been careful. But you could get pregnant. Neither one of us would want that." He flexed his hands in their bindings. "You'd best untie me now, before this goes any further."

She bit her lip thoughtfully. "There's always with-drawal."

"I believe you'll find that one a bit of a challenge, with me trussed up here like a Christmas goose."

"I'm very resourceful."

"Nora—"

Leaning forward, she closed her mouth over his, sti-fling any further objections. She'd never been the aggres-sor when it came to their kisses, and he found he liked it. She claimed his mouth with a sensual zeal that took his breath away, all the while caressing every part of him she could reach—his hair, his chest, his belly, and lower....

A low growl rose in his chest when she began to stroke him, using just the right pressure to drive him swiftly to-ward completion. He turned his head to halt the kiss, saying, "Stop!" even as he thrust upward, hungry for her touch. "Stop, Nora, stop!"

"You're right," she said with a mischievous little glimmer in her eye, scooting down a bit and reaching for his fly. "It would be better without the pants."

"Nora, no," he pleaded as she released the button and zipper over his straining erection. "Please, Nora... sweetheart...you don't know what you're doing."

"I plan to learn as I go." Nora frowned at the white boxer shorts she confronted when she got his pants open, smiling when she saw that they were the old-fashioned, button-close type. She slipped the buttons through their holes and paused, her hand hovering over him; was she working up her nerve?

His chest was pumping; his cock throbbed.

Slowly she opened his shorts, exposing that part of him that she'd kept in a state of quivering readiness for two months now. She studied it with an open fascination that he found oddly endearing. Finally she touched it lightly with a fingertip, starting when it twitched of its own accord.

Summoning a nonchalance he didn't feel, David opened his mouth to ask if she was having second thoughts, only to groan helplessly as she closed her hand around him and slid it up and down his length. His back arched off the bed; he grabbed on to the brass rod to which he was tethered, striving to keep still as she stroked him. "Nora, stop! For pity's sake!"

Her hand stilled. "You really want me to stop?"

No! "Yes," he gasped. If nothing else, he didn't want to go off in her hand, which would happen all too soon if she didn't desist. "Please, Nora. You mustn't do that to me. You mustn't touch me like that."

"All right."

Both relieved and disappointed, David sank, trembling, into the pillows and closed his eyes. He felt fabric brush against his exposed flesh and thought she must be rebuttoning his shorts, but when he opened his eyes, he found that she'd shifted so that she was straddling his hips again.

"I assume it's all right if I touch myself like that," she said as she started unbuttoning the opening to her pantaloons.

Words utterly failed him. All he could do was stare as she undid every last button. When they were all open, she slipped her fingers inside; he caught a glimpse of golden curls, but no more than that.

Quietly she said, "You did once ask me to do this." Her hand began to move, just slightly; her eyes drifted shut.

He knew what she was doing. She'd learned what excited him, what whetted his sexual appetite, and now she was using that knowledge to arouse him to the point of no return. It could work, too, he thought, watching her head tilt back slightly as she gave herself over to the pleasure of her own touch—a pleasure she'd been too self-conscious at one time to share with him. It probably still embarrassed her, which was why she'd closed her eyes, but she was doing it.

Was making love to him so important to her that she would go to such lengths to seduce him? Clearly, it was. He found that knowledge to be strangely humbling.

She looked like something out of one of those turn-of-the-century French postcards, with her loosened braids and quaintly titillating underthings, an effect magnified by the oak wainscoting and tapestries lining the walls of this room.

He could feel the tension gather in her thighs, hear her strained breathing. Her hips rocked slightly, every movement a subtle but maddening caress against his taut flesh.

It got to be too much very quickly. He trembled with

the effort it took not to thrust against her, his own breath coming harsh and fast now. With a groan of surrender he strained upward, seeking that all-too-elusive contact. "Nora," he rasped. "Untie me."

"Not yet," she breathed without opening her eyes.

"Now!" He was close, too close. His thrusts grew more urgent as his self-control slipped away. She was close, too, he saw. That telltale flush had begun to creep up her throat; little shudders coursed through her.

"Nora, untie me!" He bucked and thrashed beneath her, jerking at his restraints. "Damn it, Nora!" She didn't understand, didn't realize that he would come now, like this, if she didn't untie him. "Nora!" He felt it gathering inside him like an imminent cloudburst, felt the tightening in his extremities, and then in his hips. It would happen within seconds; he couldn't stop it now.

With a frenzied burst of strength, he wrenched at the ribbons that bound him. Lace snapped; his right hand jerked free. Nora gasped.

With his left hand still tethered, he threw her down on that side and rolled onto her, parting her legs with his. He yanked at the slit in the pantaloons, ripping it wide open. Gripping her hip with his right hand and the bedhead with his left, he drove in with a groan—*so tight, so slick*—felt something give way, heard her sharp intake of breath—*I'm sorry, Nora....*

On the razor edge of orgasm, he thrust twice more, just as savagely, his body not his to govern. Nora cried out, clutching at his shirt—*Stop, you're hurting her!*—but then he felt, deep inside her, the gripping shudders of her own climax, and with a roar, he erupted.

13

"Have I mentioned that I'm sorry for the way that happened?" David stroked Nora's hair while they lay curled up in naked tranquility beneath the billowy down comforter. She loved the prickly softness of his chest hair against her cheek, the deep reverberations of his voice in her ear.

"Only about a dozen times. I goaded you into it. Even the Lord High Control Freak has his limits. Actually, it was a thrill, seeing you lose it that way."

He sighed pensively. "I should have had more self-control. No woman should be ravished that way her first time."

She chuckled. "Every woman should be ravished that way her first time."

"Her *first* time? I might actually have hurt you, Nora. I'm still not convinced I didn't."

After that explosive lovemaking, David had withdrawn very gingerly, going pale at the sight of her blood on him. That was when the repentance had started. He'd drawn her a warm bath, chiding her for her self-consciousness when he undressed her and rhapsodizing about her beauty when she was finally standing naked in front of him.

He'd sat on floor next to the tub and talked to her while she soaked in the warm, soothing water, feeling the residual soreness between her legs gradually ease. Afterward, he'd dried her with a big, rough towel and taken her to bed, getting undressed himself before he joined her.

She didn't think she'd ever seen anything as powerfully elegant as David Waite's nude body—long and lean, but solidly muscled, an athlete's body. She'd asked him how he kept in shape, aside from that weight bench, and he'd replied that the weight bench was only to keep him fit for racquetball and tennis, which he played three or four times a week—although on Sundays he liked to pick up basketball games on the street. When he told her where, exactly, he found these games, she'd blanched.

You're not afraid of those neighborhoods? she'd asked him. He'd smiled cryptically. *I've been in far worse.*

He hadn't elaborated on that, and she hadn't pressed him. It was rare for him to reveal even that much about himself. Despite all the time they'd spent together, he still held much in reserve. He rarely offered any personal revelations, and Nora understood that she wasn't to seek them out. As a result, she knew virtually nothing about his life, aside from what he did when he was with her.

She assumed this was his way of resisting emotional involvement with her. Much as it dismayed her for him to put up this barrier, she didn't push at it, didn't try to draw him out, since doing so would have obligated her to offer revelations of her own. She couldn't imagine his reaction if she told him she'd been deceiving him about herself these past two months.

Before, when their relationship was still platonic—or relatively so—she hadn't let herself dwell overmuch on her subterfuge. They would never be together for real, she'd rationalized; he didn't want her that way. It didn't really matter.

What did it mean, if anything, that he'd offered up

these snippets of personal information just now? Was it a harbinger of revelations to come, an indication that he wanted to deepen their involvement? Perhaps making love to her *had* forced him to acknowledge his feelings for her, as Patsy had speculated. If so, Nora would have to find a way to tell him who she really was and how she had misled him all this time—an unnerving prospect, but at least all the lying would be over.

David shifted them so that they lay on their sides facing each other, their legs companionably entwined. "Ravishment is no way to initiate a virgin. There are things one can do, ways to make it more comfortable for a woman her first time."

Nora rolled her eyes. "*Comfort* wasn't high on my list of priorities."

He kissed her nose. "I should have gone slowly, been gentle, done things to make you ready, to make it less painful."

"I was hardly aware of the pain." It was only afterward that she'd felt sore, and the bath had helped.

"That's because you were on the verge of climax— purely a lucky accident, I promise you. I was much too far gone to have seen to your pleasure as I should have."

She smiled. "My pleasure was not a problem."

"No thanks to me. If I had it to do over again, I would have spent a lot more time kissing you beforehand. And touching you. I would have kissed you and touched you everywhere—" his hands roamed over her, hot and rough beneath the soft down comforter "—pleasured every inch of you, very slowly, until you were trembling with desire, until you were wet and ready and begging me to take you."

She swallowed as he plucked lightly at a nipple with one hand while the other stole between her legs. Something nudged her belly; she realized it was him. "Sounds…thorough."

"Oh, I definitely would have been thorough." Easing her onto her back, he kissed her very thoroughly indeed, then lowered his mouth to her breasts as he continued the intimate caress. He explored her gently with his long, deft fingers until her breath caught in her throat and her fists tightened in his hair. "Does this hurt?"

"No…no. Please don't stop."

He didn't stop, but he shifted position so that he could kiss her mouth again. "I would have talked to you, too," he murmured against her lips. "I would have reassured you, put you at ease. I would have told you what to expect, everything I was going to do to you."

She slid a hand between them until it met the damp tip of his erection.

"No, don't," he said breathlessly. "I won't last if you touch me, and I mean to last this time, even if it takes hours."

Hours?

"Here's what I would have told you," he said. "That I'm going to make you come this way, with my hand. And then I'm going to kiss you here…." He glided a finger along her slippery flesh until it touched, just lightly, the place where her desire was most acute. Her hips bucked; her nails dug into his shoulders. "I'll make love to you with my mouth until you're out of your mind, until you're right on that edge again, until you're screaming at me to take you."

She clung to him, spiraling closer and closer to that heart-stopping moment…

"And then I'll lie between your legs," he said, "and I'll press into you just a bit, to get you accustomed to me. And all the while I'll be touching you just like this, so you'll probably come again, but I still won't stop touching you. I won't push in any farther until you demand it, and then only another little bit, just enough to stretch you open. It will take a very long time before I'm completely inside you, and by then I'll be ready to explode. So I'll have to lie still for awhile. When I move again, it will be slowly, very slowly. I'll make it last until you're right at that peak again, by which time I'll be right there with you. I'll hold out as long as possible, but when you come, when I feel those spasms inside you and I hear you cry out and I know I did that to you, it will surely send me over the edge...."

He pushed a finger inside her, detonating her pleasure with shocking force. She heard a guttural shout—*Is that me?*—as she lost herself in sensual abandon.

David held her, whispering soothing things in her ear until the last tremors had coursed through her, and then he kissed her...first her mouth, and then her throat, her breasts, her belly, and lower....

Hours? she thought.

"HOURS..." she mumbled into his chest as she lay in his warm embrace, damp and limp and snug under the rumpled comforter.

"Hmm?" He nuzzled her hair.

"I thought that was an exaggeration."

"I never exaggerate."

"Did you learn all that stuff from the *Kama Sutra?*" she asked.

"Well...in part." He hesitated. "There's another ancient Indian text called *The Perfumed Garden* which is quite enlightening. And, of course, there was a certain amount of...practical application, as well. But believe me when I say I have never, ever, enjoyed that application as much as I do with you."

She chuckled. "Ah, yes, ever the diplomat. You've got quite the chivalrous streak, David."

"It's chivalry now, is it? Here I thought I was just a throwback to the Victorian era, and you've plopped me down in the Middle Ages."

"I can see you in your gleaming armor on your warhorse, pennants flapping, ready to do battle for God and king."

"Quite the flattering image, considering how irresponsibly I used you."

"Uh..." She sat up, holding the covers to her chest in a too-late, too-little attempt at modesty. "If you recall, I was the one using you."

"At first." He sat up as well, his expression troubled. "You were going for withdrawal, remember? You might even have managed it if I hadn't...taken matters into my own hands. When it came to the second time round, I reasoned that the damage had already been done, so to speak, but..." He raked his unruly hair off his forehead. "I don't like taking chances."

"It's not a very fertile time of the month for me."

"You can get pregnant at any time of the month. Have you ever thought about what you'd do if—"

"I'd have the baby."

He nodded, his gaze on the big tapestry covering the opposite wall, which depicted a medieval wedding feast. "I want you to know that if you do get pregnant, I'll do the right thing."

Nora pulled the comforter up over her shoulders. "The right thing? You mean..."

"Marry you," he said shortly. "To legitimize the baby."

Put like that, it sounded like some bloodless business transaction. "You'd marry me purely out of a sense of duty?"

He turned to her. "There *is* a place for duty, even today."

"Right. Of course." Had she really hoped he might declare his deeply buried feelings for her, just because she'd had sex with him? It would seem there were no real feelings to unearth. Turning away, she reached for her blouse on the chair next to the bed and pulled it on. "Duty. It's another one of those underrated, old world virtues of yours, like self-control and honor and—oh, yeah, keeping that stiff upper lip."

"Nora...?" He touched her back.

She got off the bed and reached for her pantaloons. Remembering they were torn wide open, she donned one of the petticoats instead. "Mustn't let yourself care, mustn't let on if you do."

"Is that what you think of me?" he asked quietly.

Gathering up her clothes, she turned to face him. "You're a stranger to me in so many ways, David. Maybe if you'd ever opened yourself up to me just a little, told me anything about yourself, shared anything personal, maybe then I'd know what to think of you. As it is..." She shook her head and crossed to the doorway that led to her room.

"Nora." He sprang out of bed and came up behind her, lightly massaging her back. "Stay here, Nora. You're just tired. Nothing's wrong, not really."

Her hand on the doorknob, she said, "I wish that were true."

"Nora, whatever the problem is, we can put it right."

"The problem is I'm in love with you." She squeezed her eyes closed.

His hands stopped moving. The very air between them buzzed.

"That's the problem," she said shakily, "and there's nothing I can do about it, so please don't ask me to stay and listen to you talk about...about damage being done, and duty, and doing the right thing. There's just so much I can take."

"Nora..." His hands closed around her waist.

"Please let me go." She rested her forehead against the door. "I can't do this, not tonight, not after... I can't."

He tightened his grip momentarily and then released her.

She opened the door and slipped through, locking it behind her.

HYPOCRITE, Nora admonished herself the next morning as she took in the sunrise from an iron bench overlooking the majestic, misty Hudson River. In the hotel, about a hundred yards behind her across an undulating lawn dotted with silver maples, bedraggled party goers were either hitting the sack or inhaling coffee before that ninety-minute drive back to Manhattan.

Nora tucked wind-whipped strands of hair behind her ears and shoved her hands in the pockets of the parka she wore over her sweatshirt, glad she'd thought to bring it. They'd said it would get nippy overnight, and it had. It was the kind of autumn morning when you could smell the inevitable approach of winter; it smelled clean, but cold, like snow.

Where do you get off, she rebuked herself, *calling David on the carpet for being remote, when you've been secretly glad of it all along because it meant you wouldn't have to fess up about this little scam you've been perpetrating? He who is without sin...*

It was complicated, too damn complicated. Maybe David had been the smart one all along. He'd never wanted to get emotionally involved, never wanted them to tell each other their life stories. Why couldn't she just have played by his rules? Why did she have to fall in love with him?

A bitter little huff of laughter escaped her. How could she *not* have fallen in love with him?

Footsteps crackled in the bright yellow leaves blanketing the lawn behind her, growing steadily closer. Their measured cadence suggested a masculine, long-legged stride that was very familiar to her by now.

When the footsteps paused, she said, without turning around, "I'm sorry, David. I thought it might be enough, having just part of you. But it's not enough, not nearly. I want all of you, body and soul." She took a deep breath. "Obviously, you've got different priorities, and I can't fault you for that. You never pretended to want more of me than my body. So I guess what I'm saying is...I'd really appreciate it if you'd just forget what I said last night—all of it."

"You think I'm David Waite, don't you?"

She whipped her head around. It *was* David, wearing a tweed jacket over a Shetland sweater with a wool scarf wrapped around his neck, his hair breeze ruffled, his hands shoved in the pockets of his jeans.

"An understandable mistake," he said, circling the bench to stand before her. "It happens quite a lot." He hadn't shaved that morning, and from the shadowy smears under his eyes, she suspected he'd gotten no more sleep than she had.

"The fact is, I'm David's good twin." Taking a step forward, he extended his hand. "Bob."

"Okaaay..." Nora shook his hand automatically.

"You must be Nora Armstrong."

"Uh-huh..."

He scratched his chin thoughtfully. "People get us mixed up all the time, David and I. Really gets my monkey up, if you want to know the truth. I mean, you know how he is. Who'd want to be confused with that self-righteous, antediluvian prig?"

Gets my monkey up? "Um..."

"Excuse me, mind if I join you?" he asked, gesturing to the bench.

"Oh, uh, yeah—sure." She scooted over.

He sat down a polite distance from her. "And, of course, he's a proper nit when it comes to women. Wouldn't know a good thing if it bit him on the bum. But I'll bet you know that already."

A smile tugged at her mouth.

"I honestly don't know how he got to be the evil twin, and me the good. I mean, we were brought up exactly the same. The country house, the home in London, cricket, polo, Eton, Oxford, upstairs, downstairs... If you watch public television, you know the drill."

"Uh, yeah." In her mind's eye, she saw the March-mains' palatial country estate from *Brideshead Revisited*. Was he serious? Had David really grown up in such an environment?

"David had always seemed very much a part of that world." He leaned forward and rested his elbows on his knees, studying his loosely clasped hands. "He moved through it the way we all did, with that same careless sense of entitlement. It was, and still is, a world in which it's considered bad form to take anything too seriously, and David didn't. Not that he didn't excel at things—he was quite the sportsman, and he always did well in his studies. He was like one of those nineteenth-century gentlemen of leisure who end up with display cases full of fossils and beetles and stuffed owls. But there was nothing he ever really cared deeply about."

Hearing "Bob" talk this way, Nora could almost believe he was referring to someone else entirely.

"Somehow or other, he ended up reading law at Oxford, but he really didn't have it in him to focus on that at the exclusion of everything else. He had too many other interests, primarily photography—but of course, you know that."

"Uh, no..."

He glanced at her. "That's just like him, not to tell you about the photography. He was pretty good at it—not brilliant, but workmanlike. He'd even sold a couple of pictures to the newspapers. One day he packed up his camera, walked away from Oxford and never looked back. Lived in Japan for awhile, then Indonesia, Tibet, Italy, India, Brazil...."

"What was he?" Nora asked. "A freelance photographer?"

"At first. He sold quite a few pictures in the beginning, especially in areas of the world where there was some sort of calamity happening—a volcano wiping away an entire village, widespread starvation...there's always quite a lot of that. Women and children getting massacred for no good..." He sat back, frowning out over the river, a panorama of blinding autumn-hued beauty now that the sun had risen above the horizon.

"David began to realize something," he said. "He discovered he was using his camera as a sort of shield, a way to remove himself, emotionally, from the incredible nightmares he was photographing, to distance himself from what those people—real people just like him—were actually going through. When that really sank in, he put his camera down and never picked it up again. Instead, he allowed himself to actually get involved with those people and their problems—with trying to find solutions for their predicaments, most of which were devilishly expensive. His inheritance was tapped out within a year, and then he had to look elsewhere. For the first time, he discovered something he not only cared deeply about, but actually had some natural aptitude for."

Of course. "Fund-raising," Nora said.

He turned and smiled at her. "Bingo."

"How did you...I mean, how did David end up in New York?"

"He realized there are more opportunities here than anywhere else for major international fund-raising on a scale that would really do some good. There's lots of money in this town, and Americans tend to give it rather freely—perhaps because of that whole egalitarian thing you Yanks are so keen on."

"So, is he settling down here permanently, or..."

"Oh, yes. There comes a point when one has to put down roots. And he's been quite content here—well, except for his rather grotesque love life, but you must know all about that."

"'Fraid not."

"He doesn't tell you anything, does he? Well, suffice it to say his taste in women inexplicably plummeted when he moved to New York. Until...well, he met this extraordinary woman a couple of months ago. Funny how he met her. He'd gotten so fed up with relationships that he decided to opt for something called arm candy. Do you know what that is?"

"Something to do with drugs, right?"

He smiled. "It was supposed to be a no-strings relationship—no obligations, no expectations, and most of all, no feelings. Which was just how he wanted it. But then a funny thing happened.'' He turned to look at her, his expression sobering.

Nora waited.

''He fell in love with her.''

Everything shifted; Nora had to grab on to the bench to stay grounded.

''Not that he could admit it to himself, the witless *putz*.''

''*Putz?*'' Nora choked on a burst of laughter.

''Beryl called me...called David that once. It stuck.''

The laughter bubbled out of her until her eyes stung. Or maybe it was the breeze off the river making her tear up this way. Or maybe...

''Nora?''

Through a watery haze, she saw him lean toward her, one arm stretched out along the back of the bench. He raised that hand to brush the hair off her face, his own hair fluttering over his forehead, which, along with his eyes, wide and earnest, made him look almost boyish.

''This is the part where you tell me all about yourself,'' he said. ''I want to know everything, every last detail.''

She blinked, the tears spilling hot over her cheeks. He pulled a handkerchief from his inside jacket pocket and blotted them away.

Taking a deep breath, she said, ''You're not going to like it, David.''

''It's Bob.'' He smiled. ''Just don't tell me you're really a man. I think I could handle about anything else.''

Nora tried to smile back, but she couldn't quite manage it. She fixed her gaze on the river, without really seeing it. Steeling herself, she said, ''I haven't been entirely honest with you about myself. You think I'm a model, but I'm not. You'd expected your arm candy to be a model, so I pretended that's what I was, but..."

She glanced at him. He was watching her intently.

Turning away, she said, "I make jewelry. Those pieces I wear, they're samples of my work. I made them, not some...friend. It was me all along."

After a hushed interval, he said, "Those orders you take at the functions we attend..."

"I'm trying to establish myself professionally, as a custom jeweler." It was working, too. Her business was doing so well at this point that she would be able to look for her own place soon. Turning to him, she said, "The contacts I've made at those functions have been inval..."

He was staring out over the river, his face drained of color, which made those smudges under his eyes all the more pronounced. Something in his gaze, a kind of stunned dismay, filled her with dread.

He closed his eyes, rubbed his forehead. "That's...that's why you really agreed to...date me, isn't it? Not so much to help Harlan, but so that you could promote your own—"

"It was both. David..." She touched his arm.

He shot up off the bench and stalked to the edge of the lawn, where it dropped off to the river. He kept his gaze on the ground, standing with his hands on his hips, his head shaking slightly in evident disbelief.

No, no, no. Please don't let this be happening.

She got up and took a few steps toward him. Wrapping her arms around herself, she said, "I'm sorry, David. I'm so sorry. We can work this through. I'll do whatever it takes to make up for...for deceiving you the way I did. Tell me how to earn your trust again."

"The thing about deception," he said without turning around, "is that it kills trust for good. It kills everything."

"David," she said in a wavering voice, "you said you loved me."

He turned to face her, looking as distant and forbidding as she'd ever seen him. "I didn't know you."

She closed her eyes, straining for composure, willing herself not to cry.

In a low, strained voice, he said, "Look, uh, why don't you get a ride back with Harlan?"

She opened her eyes. "David."

He clenched his jaw and looked away. "I've got to leave now. I've got to get away from here...."

"David, please..." She took a step toward him.

He turned and walked away.

14

THE PHONE STARTED RINGING as David was unlocking his apartment door. He didn't bother to hurry, having made it a point not to answer any calls for the past three days, ever since that morning at Gatwick Castle when Nora had admitted...

Don't think about it, you pathetic bastard. Get over it and let it be a lesson to you.

Except he'd thought he'd already learned his lesson, after Helena and the others. To have been sold once again on the same old dodgy manipulations was as shameful as it was devastating.

Holding on to the little brown bag he'd brought back from the corner shop—his first excursion out of the house in three days, a futile attempt to get out of himself—he took off his tweed jacket and tossed it on the little table next to the door. It immediately slipped to the floor, but he made no move to pick it up. The place was a veritable piggery lately; what difference would it make?

After the third ring, the answering machine in the bedroom kicked in: "Um, David, it's me again."

Nora. He closed his eyes, rubbed his forehead. Hortense writhed against his legs, but he ignored her.

"I guess, since you're not returning my calls, that...well, I guess I really blew it."

He walked into the bedroom, his gaze on the little gray machine next to the phone.

"I know I did." Her voice sounded rough and a little damp, as if she'd been crying. "I wanted you to know that I...I understand why you took it so hard, about me...misleading you that way, and profiting from the connections I made through you. Beryl told me—I called her this morning to tell her, you know, the truth about me. She told me about Helena Parr and those other women. David, I'm sorry. Please believe me when I say it wasn't like that with me. I really did love you. I still do."

Sitting on the edge of his unmade bed, David set the paper bag on the bedside locker and stared at it.

"For what it's worth," she said, "I think you're a great guy. If this is goodbye, I'd like to say it in person. If we could meet somewhere, just for a few minutes...I promise not to make a scene, I just can't say goodbye to an answering mach—"

David lifted the receiver. "Nora."

There was a moment of silence, then she said, "You're there."

He closed his eyes. "I can't meet you, Nora. I...couldn't bear it."

She let out a breath. "This *is* goodbye, then."

After a heavy pause, he said, "Look, Nora...one thing." He rubbed his jaw, spiky with three days' growth of beard. "If it happens that you've become pregnant, you must promise to let me know. I *will* want to marry you, so the child will have my name. You can divorce me as soon as you'd like—I'll give you whatever you want in the way of a settlement."

There came a little huff of sound, like a sad chuckle. "Chivalrous to the end. I'm not pregnant, David. I got my period yesterday."

"Right. Well, then."

"Thank you for wanting to do the right thing, though.

Despite those things I said before, I do admire that about you."

"I wish you well, Nora."

She said something teary that might have been "Goodbye," and then there came a click, followed by a dial tone.

He lifted the paper bag, opened it up. What did it mean that he'd felt vaguely disappointed when she told him she wasn't pregnant? Probably only that he was still mortifyingly in her thrall. When would he learn?

Upending the paper bag, he let the four packets of Dunhills he'd bought tumble out onto the bed, along with the receipt and the matchbooks the shopman had thrown in.

The phone rang again. He ignored it as he crumpled up the bag and threw it across the room, missing the litter bin by a foot. He'd better get his aim back before he rejoined the world, or at least before he picked up any more basketball games.

The phone rang twice more as he peeled the cellophane off one of the packets, flipped it open, shoved a cigarette between his lips and lit it.

"David, it's me, Beryl. Pick up."

The smoke scoured his lungs as he sucked it in.

"Come on, David. I tried you at work, but what's-her-name with the Jamaican accent told me you hadn't been there since last Friday. I talked to Nora this morning. She told me she thought it was over between you two. What are you, *nuts?* She's absolutely the best thing that ever happened to you, you sorry schmuck."

Coming over queer from the unaccustomed rush of nicotine, David fell back onto the bed and stared woozily at the carved moldings around the ceiling. It probably wouldn't be affecting him this way if he had anything in his stomach, but it was four in the afternoon already, and he hadn't eaten yet, although he'd been awake for almost three hours.

"All right, here's why I called. It seems to me, if you really did break things off with Nora, you might be in the market for a different flavor of arm candy—someone new."

"And pigs might start soaring through the air," David rasped, taking another, shallower drag on the cigarette. He got the smoke down without his lungs seizing up; progress.

"'Cause I've got someone in mind," Beryl said.

No, really? David blew a stream of smoke toward the ceiling.

"Patsy Crane."

He choked convulsively as his throat spasmed. Sitting up, he gave vent to a coughing fit of tubercular proportions.

"I guess you know," Beryl continued, "that Patsy gave Alec the heave-ho. Alec is beside himself. He sent her flowers, but she sent them back. He tried calling her, but she hung up on him. She's actually showing some backbone for once, and it's thrown him into a state of shock. He says he's gonna back off and give her time to cool down, but he doesn't get it. She's through with him—or at least she thinks she is. If he doesn't make some kind of meaningful gesture soon—and by meaningful I mean a little velvet box with a great big rock inside it, not a dozen roses or a whiney apology—he's gonna lose her for good."

Probably for the best, David thought.

"You're thinking that'd be for the best, but that's just because you're too steeped in your own gloom and doom right now to see what's at stake here. Alec and Patsy were made for each other. I just hope that idiot son of

mine comes to his senses before she starts dating someone else. That's where you come in."

Beryl sounded like a woman with a mission, and that
made David nervous.

"Ask her out," Beryl said. "It's the perfect way to keep
other men away from her until Alec wakes up and pops
the question. And the way I figure it, there's little risk of
you two screwing things up by getting involved for real.
There appears to be zero chemistry of that sort between
you."

Zero about summed it up. Although Patsy was pretty,
and a lovely person, she was devoid of sex appeal as far
as he was concerned. It had always, in fact, been something of a mystery to him why Alec was so hung up on
her, but then the human heart tended to be a rather un-
fathomable little organ.

"And it would benefit you, as well," Beryl said.
"You'd have a woman on your arm, so you wouldn't
have to deal with looking available."

A compelling argument, he had to admit, but you had
to do better than that when you were dealing with an
agoraphobe in training.

"So, for what it's worth," Beryl said, "that's my sug-
gestion. I think it's a good one. Take it or leave it."

Click.

David smoked his cigarette all the way down, then,
reeling with nausea, lit another off the butt and smoked
that one as well.

15

"EVENIN', MR. WAITE," said Tom as he swung open the front door of the Rialto. Noticing the dinner suit David had on under his open coat, the doorman asked, "Another one of your charity shindigs?"

David sighed. "That's right."

Tom checked his watch. "Isn't it a little early for you to be coming back from one of them? It's not even ten o'clock."

"Yes, well..." Before she'd left for Palm Beach last week, Beryl had finally talked him into asking out Patsy Crane; after several weeks of attending his functions stag, he'd been eager to discourage, at least for the time being, the interest of other women. He'd pulled himself together enough to see to his professional responsibilities; that was about all he could handle right now.

It had been Patsy's first "date" since breaking up with Alec, about whom she'd rabbited on nonstop all evening, finally bursting into tears in the car as David was taking her home. He'd held her as she wept, escorted her to her apartment and sighed with relief walking away.

It should have been Alec's shoulder she'd dampened with her tears, as he offered a litany of his sincerest mea culpas. Alec had been pining away for Patsy in utter misery this past month, during which he had, to David's knowledge, not so much as glanced in any other woman's direction.

In addition to the tedium factor, his date with Patsy had served as an excruciating reminder of how much he'd always loved being with Nora. Like Beryl and his grandmother Sunny, she'd never held back with him, never wrapped her comments in a soft blanket of politeness just to get along, as most others were wont to do. Her always diverting insights, her thunder-flash smile and that kittenish little laugh of hers had gotten him through many an otherwise stifling evening.

Just looking at her was sometimes enough. And when he'd finally been able to touch her...

Dragging a hand through his hair, David glanced toward the alcove that housed the residents' mailboxes. "Did I get my mail this morning, or...?"

"Nah, you forgot it again." Leaning against the wall, Tom pulled from his pocket a thin paperback, the cover of which portrayed a half-dressed couple in a feverish embrace.

David unlocked his mailbox, ruminating on the state of constant distraction he'd been immersed in of late. It was as if he was functioning on autopilot, just going through the motions.

"Hey, Mr. Waite," Tom called from the lobby, "if I don't see you tomorrow, have a happy Thanksgiving."

Extracting a stack of letters and junk mail from the box, he muttered, "You, too, Tom."

"Are you gonna spend the holiday with that pretty girlfriend of yours?"

David slid on his reading glasses as he emerged from the alcove, sorting through his post. "That's been over for the better part of a month now."

"Hunh. Come to think of it, I haven't seen her around lately. I thought you'd been lookin' pretty glum, but I didn't know you got dumped. Boy, they can really stick it to you, huh? You're better off without her. Beautiful broads like that, they're just lookin' for Daddy Warbucks."

David frowned at his mail, finding the bad-mouthing of women distasteful in general, but especially ill at ease to hear Nora spoken of as if she were just another shallow gold digger. She had her faults, God knew, but at least she was trying to make her own way, not latch onto a sugar daddy. "It wasn't like that, Tom. Actually..." He couldn't believe he was discussing such personal matters with his doorman. Welcome to America. "I'm the one who broke things off."

"Seriously?" Tom guffawed in astonishment. "What are you, *nuts?"*

Déjà vu.

"I'm not kiddin'," Tom said, his novel forgotten. "I mean, look at her compared to that dress designer chick you used to come in here with, who had to be, if you'll pardon the expression, the biggest bitch goddess in New York, and we know how to grow 'em here."

"If you've finished this fascinating little postmortem on my love life," David said, edging toward the elevator, "I think I'll just—"

"What I said before, about the other one, the blonde, dumpin' you for Daddy Warbucks, that was just talk. You know that, right? I mean, I was just tryin' to make you feel better, guy to guy. It didn't mean nothin'."

"Thank you for the male bonding experience. Now if you don't mind—"

"The thing is," Tom persisted, "what with the way you been mopin' around all this time, you don't seem real happy about this breakup, even if you *were* the one who called it quits. Maybe this is one of those cases where you can patch things up."

David gritted his teeth. "There's no way to put this one right, Tom."

"Is that how she feels?"

"Real life," David said, growing impatient, "isn't like those books of yours."

Tom snorted. "Don't I know it. Why do you think I read them?"

"It couldn't, by any chance, be for the sex," David suggested aridly.

"Hell, no!" Tom declared, looking genuinely affronted. "Yeah, all right, a little. But mostly it's 'cause everything always turns out all right in the end."

David stabbed the elevator button. "They're fairy tales," he said contemptuously.

Tom opened up his book, muttering something as the elevator doors whooshed open.

"What's that?" David asked, holding the door open with his hand.

Tom looked up at him. "I said they'd be fairy tales if the happy ending just, like, came outa nowheres. You know, if, like, a fairy godmother made it happen, some bogus crap like that. But it's the guy and the girl. They make it happen." Sticking his nose back in his book, he added, "Both of them."

THE FIRST THING David did after closing his apartment door behind him was to pour himself a stiff Scotch on the rocks, which he downed in one gulp. Only then did he shed his overcoat and dinner jacket, yank off his bow tie and kick off his shoes. He braced both arms on the mantelpiece, studying the wood stacked on the hearth and weighing whether the comforts of a fire would be worth the trouble of building and lighting it.

In the end, he pushed away from the mantel and went

into the bathroom, where he spent about five minutes meditating on Nora's little feathered and jeweled hair pick, which still occupied one of the slots of his toothbrush holder.

He picked it up, something he hadn't allowed himself to do this past month, and twirled it slowly, watching the little jewels glint in the harsh overhead light. Opening his hand, he brushed the feathers across his palm, kindling a deep, hot shiver that went right into his chest.

His next breath caught in his throat. "Bloody hell." He went to put the hair pick back, but changed his mind and held on to it.

Returning to the living room, he stood in front of the wall of pictures above the Barcelona chair, contemplating the little Indian painting of the couple making love in the lotus position, his gaze riveted on the woman's eyes. Drowsy with desire and focused intently on her lover, they looked for all the world like Nora's eyes when he'd been inside her that second time, when he'd slowed down and done it right. They were the eyes of a woman transported; they were the eyes of a woman in love.

He hadn't seen her in nearly a month, hadn't spoken to her since that final, agonizing phone call. That was for the best, of course—a clean break and all that. He shouldn't want to gaze upon her, shouldn't crave the sound of her voice.

Get over it. What's the matter with you?

Pouring himself another Scotch, he sat on the Barcelona chair to nurse it while he pondered the problem of how to put Nora Armstrong out of his mind. Hortense leapt onto his lap and started nesting, mauling his testicles in the process, as was her special talent. He teased her with the hair pick; she gave it one or two lethargic swats and settled down, turning that resonant purr of hers up to full volume.

He must concentrate on his business, that was it. He must plan some new charity event, something exciting and different—something for those young philanthropists Harlan had proven himself so adept at wooing. Surprisingly, Harlan hadn't called him to pitch any new ideas since the Halloween party, but that didn't mean David couldn't propose some himself. He should call him; they'd brainstorm.

Setting aside his half-empty glass and scooping the indignant Hortense off his lap, he went over to his rolltop desk and flipped through the Rolodex until he found the card labeled Harlan Armstrong. There were two numbers scrawled on it, one for his apartment and one for his cell phone.

He lifted the handset from his fax machine and punched out the apartment number. It was late; Harlan would be home. If Nora happened to answer the phone, well, that couldn't be helped. It wouldn't be as if David had deliberately sought her out. They could exchange pleasantries; he could be civil even in the face of what she'd done to him. It was all water under the bridge at this point.

His heart rattled as the phone rang once, twice...

"Hello?" It was Harlan.

Swallowing down his idiotic disappointment, he said, "Harlan. David Waite here. I hope it's not too late to call."

"Piss off, David."

Click.

David stood with the receiver to his ear for several seconds before it sank in that Harlan had... *Bloody hell.* "The little bugger hung up on me."

He redialed the number.

Harlan answered with a testy sigh. "'Piss off'—that's American for roast in hell."

"I know what it means, Harlan—some thick-witted colonist stole the expression from us. What I don't know is why you're being so damnably hostile." It was especially bizarre and unexpected given his former solicitude.

"Ask Nora. Oh, wait a minute, you can't, because you cut her out of your life for no good reason. I *knew* you'd screw her over, you cold-blooded bastard. I never should have set the two of you up together."

"Back up," David said, gesturing with the hair pick, although there was nobody there to see. "No good reason? You must be joking. She'd been playing me around, as you're very well aware. She used me."

"You used her, too. That whole arm candy thing?"

"That was different," David said. "That was on the up and up—between us, at any rate. What she did to me was deceitful—passing herself off as a model, when—"

"Now who's being thick-witted?"

"What's that supposed to mean?"

"Who do you think put her up to that?" Harlan asked. "She only agreed to the arm candy thing in the first place for me, much against her better judgment. And the only reason she pretended to be a model was because I insisted on it. After the Waldorf thing, when you enlisted her for the steady, ongoing gig, she *begged* me to tell you the truth. She *pleaded* with me, said she couldn't live a lie, that it was unconscionable. I talked her into it for *my* sake. *Mine.* Any benefit to her was purely secondary, and it was never, *ever* important enough to her to justify the deception."

Harlan actually sounded winded after this vehement

monologue. David pulled the chair out and sat down as he groped for some response.

"There are so many ironies here," Harlan said, "that I hardly know where to begin. Two gigantic ones stand out, though. Irony number one is that I engineered this whole masquerade for the sake of my career. Nora was just as much a victim of it as you were, and yet she's the one who takes the heat for it, while you end up trying to throw me even more business! I assume that's why you called."

David sighed and rubbed his forehead. "And irony number two?"

"You're gonna love this one. Irony number two is Nora *thinks this whole fiasco is her fault!* She blames herself, can you believe it? Totally exonerates you for any wrongdoing, says it was perfectly understandable why you dumped her. The way she sees it, she lied for two months to the only man she's ever loved. Why *wouldn't* he be outraged? She doesn't buy that it's really my fault for coercing her into it, 'cause she says she's a grown-up and a free agent and she knew better, but she did it, anyway. As far as she's concerned, she blew it, plain and simple. Must make you feel great, really vindicated, having her come right out like that and say, 'He was right and I was wrong.'"

David felt a lot of things right now, but "great" wasn't one of them.

"Don't get the idea," Harlan said, "that just because she blames herself she's taking this whole thing on the chin. In the beginning, when you wouldn't return her calls, it was like her insides had been ripped right out. For about a week after that, she was a *zombie*, except when she was bawling her eyes out. I'd never seen her like that, ever. She's better now, but still just an open sore, emotionally. You have no idea what I've been going through this past month, knowing this whole thing was my fault, that I did this to her—with a little help from you, you rigid, judgmental, unforgiving, arrogant, kidney-eating limey prick.''

"Right. You know, Harlan, some of this has actually been elucidating. Not that it excuses what happened, but it does explain a few things. May I ask why you didn't think to ring me up and share this with me before now?''

"Actually, what I thought about doing was coming over to your place with half a dozen leather boys swinging baseball bats and chains. Nora wouldn't let me. No sense of drama.''

David gazed forlornly at his drink, on the other side of the room.

"And she made me promise not to phone you,'' Harlan added, "not if I was gonna, you know...''

"Accuse me of eating kidneys?''

"She didn't mind if I continued to work with you—she wanted me to—but she made me swear I wouldn't call you and get into it about the whole break up.''

"And yet you have.''

"Ah, but I didn't call you. You called me, which means all bets are off. To what do I owe the honor, anyway?''

"Would you believe I was in the mood for a good tongue-lashing?''

"Sorry, fella, but you're not my type.''

"I *was* actually hoping we could do business again together.''

"Oh, yeah. Sure. *When hell freezes over.*''

"Oh, come on, Harlan—''

"Hear me out, David. I don't need your business. I don't want your business. I wouldn't take your business if the only alternative was scrubbing the spit off subway platforms.''

''I'm sorry to hear that, Harlan. I...'' David sank back in his chair, closed his eyes. ''Look, is Nora there? I'd like to talk to her.''

''You're out of luck, pal. She's gone.''

He sat up, his eyes snapping open. ''Gone? Not back to...''

''Ohio? Nah—she's still crazy about this city. She got her own place, though. Moved out two weeks ago.''

''Where? Here in Manhattan?''

''What do you care? You had your chance with her.''

''Come on, Harlan,'' David said, slipping the hair pick in his trouser pocket and plucking his favorite vintage Mont Blanc pen out of the pencil jar. ''What's her phone number?''

''Area code two-one-two, five-five-five, eat me.''

Click.

Turning, David hurled the Mont Blanc across the room. It shattered against the opposite wall, spraying ink.

Bzzt! The doorman's signal from downstairs broke the ensuing silence.

Swearing and clawing at his hair, David stalked to the intercom panel and pressed the button. ''What.''

Tom's staticky voice said, ''Mr. Van Aucken's on his way up.''

Alec? He always called first. ''Great.'' Releasing the button, David slumped against the wall.

He could get Nora's number from Information, but it was probably a bad idea. Nothing substantive had changed; Nora had still lied to him for two months, regardless that she'd felt conflicted about it. Why draw things out painfully when they'd already managed the coveted clean break?

Still, if he could just hear her voice one more time...

There came a rapping on the door. David opened it.

A fist slammed into his face, sending him sprawling.

What? David rolled aside just as Alec aimed a foot at his midsection, then wobbled and fell, cursing thickly. He reeked of whiskey.

David leapt to his feet. "Alec, what the—"

"Come 'ere!" Alec demanded, scrambling unsteadily as he tried to rise. "Come 'ere an' fight me like a man, you back-stabbing sack of—"

"Look, Alec," David said, backing out of his way as Alec swung crazily, eyes wild and unfocused. "I don't know what this is about, but you're obviously potted. Don't you think you should just—"

"I think I should punch your freakin' lights out for goin' behin' my back with Patsy."

Oh, yes. This is a splendid new development.

Edging around the coffee table, David held his hands up in a gesture of appeasement. "Alec, I'm not trying to steal Patsy from you." He thought it best not to mention that Patsy had broken up with Alec a month ago, and therefore could not, technically, be stolen from him, and that he, David, found Patsy almost completely lacking in sexual allure.

"*Bullshit!*" Alec screamed, lunging for him. "I saw you!"

David stepped aside, wincing as Alec jettisoned over the coffee table, ending up facedown on the straw floor mat. A silver hip flask slid out of the inside pocket of his rumpled sport coat. "Fight me," he moaned, struggling to rise. "Fight me, you gutless bastard."

"Alec." Squatting next to his friend, David pushed him

back down with a hand on his shoulder. "I have no intention of fighting you." Alec had gotten in that first, surprise punch—David's jaw throbbed—but if David were to actually fight back, he'd lay Alec out in about a nanosecond.

"*Fight me!*" Alec wailed, slamming both fists onto the mat. "*Why won't you fight me?*"

"I'm not making a play for Patsy, Alec."

"I saw you! I was there tonight, across the street from her building. I saw you with her."

"You staked out her apartment? You've been *spying* on her?"

"Jus' tonight. Mother called me from Palm Beach this morning. She heard a rumor Patsy had started seein' someone."

Beryl. David rolled his eyes. *Of course.*

"I couldn't believe it when I saw you bring her home," Alec slurred. "I thought you were my friend! How could you do this to me?"

"Listen to me, Alec."

"Go to hell!" Alec struggled to get up.

David grabbed a fistful of his friend's hair and leaned in close. "This is your mother's doing. We both played right into her hands."

"What are you talkin' about?"

"She sold me on dating Patsy—strictly as arm candy, mind you—by claiming it was to keep other men at bay until you were ready to make your move. In reality, she was hoping to force your hand by making you jealous—hence her phone call this morning."

Alec closed his eyes and went limp, swearing under his breath. "That woman is gonna be the death of me."

"You?" Releasing Alec, David stood and rubbed his

aching jaw, only to discover his lip was split, as well. "I'm just glad you don't carry a handgun."

"Sorry about that, man." Grabbing on to the coffee table, Alec hauled himself awkwardly to his feet. "I went kinda nuts, I guess. It's just that I love Patsy so much. The thought of losin' her to you...to anybody..."

"See, the thing I fail to grasp, Alec, is why you were nailing half the women in New York, if it was Patsy you loved all along."

"Are you sayin' I din' really love her?" Alec asked, his tone going from conciliatory to belligerent in a heartbeat. "What do you know about love? You've got a freakin' ice cube in your chest."

"If only that were true," David muttered, turning away.

Alec followed him into the kitchen. David got a bag of frozen peas out of the freezer, pressing it against his jaw as he sat on a stool at the central island.

"It's true, all right," Alec said, claiming the other stool. "Only a soulless android would let a woman like Nora go without a fight. I don't care what you think she did to you. What matters is the two of you connected like no two people I've ever seen, an' you kicked her out of your life just 'cause she's human and flawed like the rest of us. Well, I'm not about to let Patsy slip through my fingers. I'm gonna marry her."

"It would appear your mother really does always get her way." David pulled his cigarettes from his back pocket and lit one.

"Always. You're smoking again, huh? I guess you didn't hear what they said on 'Sixty Minutes.'"

"Never watch the show. When you say you're going to marry Patsy, you mean you're going to *ask* her to marry you. There's no guarantee she'll accept, not after...well, what she's put up with from you."

"I'm a changed man," Alec said, sounding almost sober. "I'll have to make her believe that. Mother says it's a good idea, when you're asking a woman to marry you, to have a really spectacular engagement ring on hand as a gesture of good faith—especially if you're not sure what her answer will be. She says I ought to go to the diamond district, that they've got the finest stones in the world there if you know what to look for, but I thought it might be more romantic to take her to Tiffany's."

"Tiffany's makes beautiful things," David said thoughtfully.

"But..." Alec prompted.

Setting aside the bag of peas, David withdrew the hair pick from his pocket. "So does Nora."

Alec shook his head, grinning incredulously. "You're trying to send business her way, even though you're convinced she done you wrong? Anyone ever tell you you're chivalrous to a fault?"

David smiled as he twirled the hair pick. "Funny you should mention that."

16

"GOOD AFTERNOON, Miss Armstrong," said the maître d' at the entrance to Tavern on the Green's Crystal Room. "I haven't seen you in some time. Will Mr. Waite be joining you for lunch today?"

"No, um...I'm meeting someone else. Alec Van Aucken." She scanned the familiar dining room, now festively decorated for the holidays, but saw no sign of Alec. "I guess he's not here yet."

"I'm sure he'll be along shortly. Would you like a table near the Christmas tree?"

"Sure," she replied, adding a heartfelt "Holy cow" when she got a good look at the tree. It was easily twelve or fourteen feet tall, and alive with twinkling lights.

The maître d' led her to a table next to it and pulled out a chair for her. "Enjoy your lunch."

Setting her pocketbook on the table, Nora withdrew the little blue velvet pouch containing the engagement ring Alec had commissioned for Patsy. The point of this luncheon meeting was for him to inspect and, hopefully, approve her handiwork. She just wished he'd chosen some other restaurant—*any* other restaurant—for this transaction.

Too many memories, she thought, looking around. She and David used to eat here three or four times a week while they were dating. He probably still came here for business lunches, but this was the first time she'd set foot in the place since they'd stopped seeing each other.

What would she do if she looked across the room and saw him sitting with a client? How would she feel?

Oh, to see him just one more time...

It was the last thing she should want.

Yet, some days, it was all she wanted, all she thought about.

Nora cradled the velvet pouch in her hand, savoring the solid little weight inside. She was proud of the ring, but a little anxious about Alec's reaction to it. It wasn't your run-of-the-mill engagement ring. Would he like it?

Would Patsy? Her tastes tended to be conservative. Maybe it hadn't been such a good idea, Alec giving Nora carte blanche to create such an important piece of jewelry.

Just use your imagination, Alec had said when Nora had asked him what he'd wanted. *Create a masterwork, your vision of the most incredible ring ever. Nothing's too good for Patsy. I've got a lot to make up for.* He'd provided the stone himself, an utterly flawless, two-carat, oval-cut diamond that had cost him God knew how much, then paid for her work in advance. That had been ten days ago. All that remained now was to have him okay the ring and come up with an inscription.

Hearing someone at the next table say, "Look, the first snow of the season, and with the sun shining," Nora turned toward the glass wall nearest her, which looked out on the Crystal Garden. In the bright, cold sunshine, the light-festooned trees resembled spun sugar confections being dusted by yet more sugar in the form of a glittering mist of snowflakes.

Those trees remind me of you, David had told her the first time they'd come here, *and of that jewelry you're always wearing, which suits you so well. Nature rendered sublime....*

The memory squeezed her throat. Out of all the restaurants in New York, Alec had had to pick on this one.

"Hello, Nora."

Nora turned to find David standing over her, quietly handsome in a gray suit and tie.

She stared at him, her heart like a fist in her chest. "David. Hi."

"May I join you?" he asked.

"Ah. Well...I'm meeting Alec." Indicating the little velvet sack, she said, "He commissioned an engagement ring for Patsy."

There was a slight pause, then David said, "I know. I'd still like to join you." Without waiting for her consent, he pulled out the chair kitty-corner from hers and sat.

He knew? Alec must have told him he would be meeting Nora here today. Was it possible David had come here deliberately to see her? She chastised herself for the foolish surge of hope this possibility inspired. Wanting to talk to her, just for old times' sake, wasn't the same as wanting to give them another chance.

"How have you been?" he asked.

"Um...well, I have my own place now. It's in a real nice pre-war building on the Upper West Side. And my business is..." She hesitated. Her business, or rather, her lies about it, had been the reason they'd broken up.

"I hear it's skyrocketing," he said with a smile.

She smiled back, relieved. "It's been incredible—much better than I'd anticipated."

"And other than that, how are you?" he asked.

A young man came by and filled two glasses with ice water. She took a slow sip. "Not so good. You?"

"Not so good. I, uh...started smoking again."

"No. Oh, David..."

"But then I flushed them all down the toilet about a week and a half ago, so I've been nicotine-free since then. It's for good this time."

"I'm glad to hear it."

His gaze drank her in. "You look beautiful, Nora—as always."

She arched a skeptical eyebrow. Wearing an unremarkable black sweater and skirt with no jewelry and little makeup, her hair in a simple braid down her back, she felt entirely—and safely—plain.

David, on the other hand, was as coolly elegant as ever, in a suit the color of burnished steel and that silver necktie of his. The last time she'd seen him in that tie, he'd used it to lash her hands to the daybed before driving her—driving both of them—into a frenzy of desire.

Was it really possible that the urbane and ultracivilized man looking across the table at her right now was the same man who'd ravished her with such savage abandon the night she'd turned the tables on him and tied *him* to the bed? Was this the man who'd made love to her, slow and sweet, for hours afterward, who'd declared his love the next morning...

Only to take it back almost immediately. *I don't know you.*

Pointing to the blue velvet pouch, he said, "Mind if I take a look?"

"Not at all."

Donning his reading glasses, he opened the pouch and slid the ring into his palm.

"Oh, Nora..." He held the ring up, turning it this way

and that, the diamond flashing in the sunlight from the window. "You've outdone yourself. It's...phenomenal."

She couldn't suppress her proud smile. *She* thought it was phenomenal, but then her work wasn't to everyone's taste.

It had taken her days just to perfect the design—a golden circle of minuscule interwoven vines growing around and partly over the spectacular diamond. The work had been highly detailed and time-consuming, and she'd had to start over twice, but the final result was just what Alec had wanted—a masterwork. She'd photographed it from every angle for her portfolio; those pictures were all she would have of it once she handed it over to Alec.

"I told him I could make a pair of wedding rings to go with it," she said. "Patsy's would fit together with the engagement ring—the vines would sort of intersect."

David had a faraway look in his eyes as he studied the ring. "I can't imagine why I never realized it was you all along, making these extraordinary things. They're so like you—so much a part of the earth, yet so far above it."

Nora had no idea what to make of his presence here, or his reflective, almost wistful demeanor. Seeing him again was, on the one hand, deeply gratifying, on the other, heartbreaking.

"There's no inscription," he said, peering at the inner surface of the band.

"Alec is going to give it to me today."

David set the ring on the velvet pouch and took off his reading glasses. "Alec isn't coming, Nora."

"What do you mean? He said—"

"I've got the inscription for you." He withdrew a

folded sheet of lined paper from his inside coat pocket and handed it to her.

She unfolded it. Written in blue-black fountain-pen ink in David's distinctive masculine hand were the words *Nora: Why Not Take All of Me? David.*

Nora stared unblinkingly at the sheet of paper, rereading the words over and over, not trusting herself to glean a meaning from them.

"Is it too long?" he asked. "You could inscribe just the first letter of every word, if it would help. You and I would know what it meant."

You and I? she thought dizzily, looking up and meeting his gaze. *There's a you and I?*

Leaning toward her, David said, "The ring isn't for Patsy, Nora. I asked Alec to order it for me—to give to you. He got Patsy's ring from Tiffany's—she's really more a Tiffany's kind of girl—and he already gave it to her, and she accepted it, and... I'm rambling. It's because I'm nervous as hell."

David Waite? Nervous?

He ran a hand through his neatly combed hair, leaving it slightly mussed. "I bought the diamond from a broker Beryl recommended in the diamond district. See, it's her opinion that a man should have a ring on hand when he proposes—a really outstanding ring—especially if he's not too sure where he stands, and there seemed a certain merit to that line of thought. But, of course, you only wear your own jewelry, so I wasn't about to get *your* ring at Tiffany's. I, uh, I guessed at your ring size. I assume it can be made larger or smaller if..."

"No," she said dazedly. "It's my size, but...David, I don't understand...."

"Alec said something the other day. He said I was

chivalrous to a fault. It occurred to me that I'm lots of
things to a fault. Honor, duty, self-control, all those ster-
ling qualities I take such overweening pride in...they've
got a flip side, and that's self-righteousness. After...Helena and all that, it was hard for me to keep
things in perspective. There was a certain amount of
plain old fear operating, and it made me overreact. That's
not an excuse, just an explanation."

"I gave you plenty of reason to react the way you did."

"No, I judged you harshly, far too harshly. I was an
ass—rigid, imperious, condescending...." He smiled
wryly. "Feel free to jump in at any time. I don't seem to
be able to make my mouth stop working."

"I...I'm just in a state of shock. I'm having a hard time
absorbing all of this."

"That's because I'm confusing you by nattering on this
way. I haven't shut up long enough to actually propose."
He drew in a deep breath, as if bracing himself. "You
know I've never been much for public displays, but one
does want to do the thing properly."

With a self-conscious glance around the enormous,
crowded dining room, he rose from his chair, lowered
himself to one knee before her and took her hands in his.
The chatter of the other patrons turned to whispers and
then faded away. The muffled clink of silverware on
china tapered off and ceased as every person in the restaurant turned to watch them in hushed silence.

Quietly, earnestly, he said, "I love you, Nora, with all
my heart. I'm sorry for being such an idiot, and I'm begging you not to hold it against me."

Her eyes pricked with tears. Through the wavering
sheen, she saw his imploring, almost desperate expression. He had to be aware of their rapt audience, but he

held her gaze as if they were the only two people in the room.

"Be a bigger person than I was," he pleaded in a low voice raw with emotion. "Forgive me. Please."

She nodded, tears coursing in hot little rivulets down her cheeks. "If you'll forgive me."

"It's already done." Picking up the ring, he said, "Marry me, Nora. I need you so much. I don't want to live without you."

Her throat so tight she could hardly get the words out, she said, "Yes. Yes. Of course I'll marry you."

The room erupted in applause as David took her left hand in his and slid the ring onto her finger. Pressing her palm to his lips, he kissed it, whispering, "Thank you...thank you."

When he looked up at her, his own eyes were shimmering. Standing, he drew her to her feet and gathered her in his arms.

Cheers joined the applause as they kissed, long and deep, holding each other as if they never meant to let go, ever. As if they were one with each other at last, body and soul....

Because, of course, they were.

MILLS & BOON®

Makes any time special™

Mills & Boon publish 29 new titles every month. Select from...

Modern Romance™   **Tender Romance**™

Sensual Romance™

Medical Romance™   **Historical Romance**™

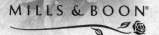

Together for the first time
3 compelling novels by
bestselling author

PENNY JORDAN

The *Bride's* BOUQUET

One wedding — one bouquet —
leads to three trips to the altar

Published on 22nd September

MILLS & BOON®

0010/116/MB6

FREE

2 BOOKS
AND A SURPRISE GIFT!

We would like to take this opportunity to thank you for reading this Mills & Boon® book by offering you the chance to take TWO more specially selected titles from the Sensual Romance™ series absolutely FREE! We're also making this offer to introduce you to the benefits of the Reader Service™ —

- ★ FREE home delivery
- ★ FREE monthly Newsletter
- ★ FREE gifts and competitions
- ★ Exclusive Reader Service discounts
- ★ Books available before they're in the shops

Accepting these FREE books and gift places you under no obligation to buy; you may cancel at any time, even after receiving your free shipment. Simply complete your details below and return the entire page to the address below. *You don't even need a stamp!*

YES! Please send me 2 free Sensual Romance™ books and a surprise gift. I understand that unless you hear from me, I will receive 4 superb new titles every month for just £2.40 each, postage and packing free. I am under no obligation to purchase any books and may cancel my subscription at any time. The free books and gift will be mine to keep in any case.

T0ZEC

Ms/Mrs/Miss/Mr ....Initials ....
BLOCK CAPITALS PLEASE

Surname ....

Address ....

....

....Postcode ....

Send this whole page to:
UK: FREEPOST CN81, Croydon, CR9 3WZ
EIRE: PO Box 4546, Kilcock, County Kildare (stamp required)

Offer valid in UK and Eire only and not available to current Reader Service subscribers to this series. We reserve the right to refuse an application and applicants must be aged 18 years or over. Only one application per household. Terms and prices subject to change without notice. Offer expires 30th June 2001. As a result of this application, you may receive further offers from Harlequin Mills & Boon Limited and other carefully selected companies. If you would prefer not to share in this opportunity please write to The Data Manager at the address above.

Mills & Boon® is a registered trademark owned by Harlequin Mills & Boon Limited.
Sensual Romance™ is a registered trademark used under license.